The quote from Dr. Emanuel Bronner, in the story *Rain Dogs*, appears courtesy of the Bronner family.

The reference to the quotes from Colin Powell and Condoleezza Rice, in the story *No Such Thing As Monsters*, are from http://www.informationclearinghouse.info/article6456.htm

Reference to the story of the unrequited widowed husband in *Love Anything*... is from the files of weirdasianews.com.

The quote from C.S. Lewis' The Four Loves in *Love Anything*... appears courtesy Harcourt Books' Permission department.

Published by Veracity Systems,
Copyright © 2013 Veracity Systems
P.O. Box 671, Stockbridge, GA 30281

Cover art by Corey Barksdale, Copyright ©2013
www.coreybarksdale.com

ISBN 978-0-615-91968-3

Six Senses and the subtitle *Perception Is A Choice*, Copyright ©2013

For more information go to www.scombs.com

SIX SENSES

Perception is a choice

S. Combs

To Tina Sabrina Combs-Molock
For being a mother
when there was illness,
For being a father
when there was absence,
For being a sister,
by birth
And for being a best friend
…cause you wanted to be.

SIX SENSES

Perception is a choice

S. Combs

EXPOSITION

I began writing stories for this book as part of an assignment for a creative writing class. Over time, as the stories and the characters evolved, the idea to put these stories together and redevelop them based on a common theme quickly formed.

Six stories, themed around each of our major senses, relay tales of tragedy, failure, and resilience as characters from various backgrounds and different paths discover the fledgling power, within all of us, to control the future and create our own destiny.

Four Eyes

Insanity is often defined as doing the same thing over and over but expecting a different result. This story is about changing the path but not the goal and achieving success. Some times that change is voluntary and other times we are forced by external circumstances to alter our strategy.

Regrets of Indulgence

Being raised by a single mother but mostly by a deeply religious southern grandmother, my sister and I were sheltered from many things. Sometimes, we were even kept away from what was 'good'. Often, we were exposed to only one side of things. For example, take food: What we were accustomed to always tasted the best until our lives were seasoned with something different or some circumstance forced us to realize that what we thought was complete and the best, was actually bland and incomplete. Sometimes, our social experiences in life transpire the same way.

The Variegated Valley
Just because we are lacking in a certain ability in a relationship, friendship, or any agreement, does not mean that we cannot achieve that specific goal without that ability. We sometimes have to rely on other perceptive powers or other strengths to achieve the same goals as other people around us. We are not made the same, so some of us have to use alternative viewpoints or methods to succeed at the same aspect.

There's No Such Thing as Monsters
Making decisions for a fulfilling life, based on media persuasion, often leads to discontent. We are taught from a young age to not believe everything we hear. What else is there to say?

Rain Dogs
Sometimes the things we think are lost are only misplaced. Being lost and being misplaced are actually two different things: Just because something is misplaced doesn't mean it can't be readjusted or redirected.
If you misplace something, it is somewhere within your possession, but you can't put your finger on it...example: you misplace your car keys when you come into the house....you might not have put them on the hook, but you KNOW they are somewhere within your house.
If you have lost something, you have no idea where it is and it cannot be located because you have lost track of it permanently... Example: You left the house with a $10 bill in your pocket, and when you go to retrieve it to pay for

something it is gone, and you have no idea where it is and when it fell from your pocket.

Love Anything and Your Heart will Be Broken
Many times, stumbling blocks of our past prevent us from moving peacefully into our future lives. Moving forward, even letting go, may require us to 'conquer' our past, learn from it, and take from it the positive parts gained. Experience does not teach us. Reflecting on the experience is how we learn.

I hope that you enjoy.

Six Senses (Contents)

The definition of insanity is looking at things the same way over and over, and expecting a different result...
"So, I wear these thick glasses now, I hate them, but I see better, but I see more."

Four Eyes
(Sight)

A satisfied grin hung upon her face as her eyes slowly opened, focusing on the fiery pink negligee lying on the floor beside her bed. The smile faded before it could ever be savored. Turning to reach over, to caress the broad chest which had pressed against hers the night before, she found, once again, he was gone. "At least the night was wonderful," she consoled herself. *I'll text him a kiss or smile*, she thought. But that intention faded quicker than her wakening grin. She knew she could not. She knew his phone, the phone she called, was off by now, and that he was home… with his wife.

Sitting up quickly, her mid back length black hair swung wildly over her shoulders as she buried her butter pecan colored face in her hands and this time managed to hold back the tears. "Jasmine, you're stupid, stupid! So stupid! Why?" she yelled at herself. "Again and again!"

The sun was coming in brightly through the blinds now. *I guess he beat the sun home*, she surmised. Downstairs, she found Malcolm and Kiara still asleep on the floor in front of the television.

"They slept down here all night?" she demanded from her sister, cooking in the kitchen. Alicia, her nineteen year old sibling gave no answer. She only whipped the spoon in the pot even harder.

"Did you hear me?" Jasmine yelled.

"Yeah," Alicia snapped, "they did!"

Off guard and confused, Jasmine stared at her sister's inflamed eyes. "What's your problem?"

"Nothing," Alicia whispered, looking down and stirring the pot again.

"WHAT IS WRONG?"

"You are! You and your crap!" Alicia snarled.

Jasmine sighed, "Here we go! Listen…"

"No you listen! You go from guy to guy and bring a new guy around these kids…"

"Tremaine is different!" Jasmine cut her off. "And I don't go from guy to guy!"

"How is he different, Jasmine? How? Is it 'cause yall went out some where on a date BEFORE you let him hit? Or did this one say he WASN'T leaving his wife?"

"Whatever! You are too young to understand," Jasmine scoffed. "It's not like that."

"It is Jasmine! And then you bring all these men around your kids... around your DAUGHTER!"

With that comment, Jasmine's worn soft brown eyes began to mirror the flames of her sister's. "You don't know anything, Alicia! He's a good man, just in a difficult situation. Even momma says I need to hold onto a man no matter what and wait for…"

"Hello? Is momma happy with a man? Does she even have a man worth anything? No! She just has all five of us with different baby daddies! She…"

"Just stop! Stop please," Jasmine gritted, turning away. Then her eyes, peering through welling tears, landed upon her daughter's puzzled expression staring back at her. "Hey baby. You awake? You want something to eat?"

Kiara nodded, then a smile appeared on the two year old's little face, benighted to all the yelling. Kneeling, Jasmine cradled her tightly, making Kiara smile harder, but making Jasmine's tears finally break free. *What are you doing, Jasmine?* she screamed in her thoughts, gritting her teeth and squeezing her baby. *So stupid, so stupid!*

* * * *

It was a cool Friday afternoon in mid November, 1999. Jasmine walked into the local Food Max to pick up groceries for the kids and herself, along with the other food needed to prepare the meal for the meeting on Saturday. *Someday*, she thought, *I'm not gonna be preparing food just for the weekends but possibly for an entire week!* She sighed at the work that would entail. Then, she smiled hard, very hard. She had come so far. She had gained so much. Maybe not more than what had been lost but still, a new day was dawning for Jasmine Chandler.

Still smiling, she made her way down the canned food isle. She thought of the women she would meet the next day and how at each meeting she had learned to control her emotions a little better. *Maybe this time, they won't have to stop in the middle of their story because of my crying! Maybe I'll just hold myself to only one box of tissue!* She chuckled so loudly that an elderly lady in the isle ahead spun around and clutched her chest! "Oh, I'm so sorry! Did I scare you?"

"Well, a little," smiled the woman. "You must be really happy about something."

"Oh yes Ma'am. Just to be alive makes me happy!"

The old woman nodded in agreement and as Jasmine turned around she was struck with the beautiful face of a tall dark stranger.

"Excuse me, but you might want to watch that," He spoke in a soothing tone.

"Ah, um," she stuttered, "what do you mean?"

"That laughing, you know, that can be contagious," he smiled. His eyes seemed so comforting to her.

Okay Jasmine, she thought, *don't loose it just because he looks good. Use your head*. "Yeah," she said as she turned and browsed through the cans on the shelf, "that can be a good thing though."

"Do you have a big family?"

"No. Why do you ask?" she wondered, turning towards him again, trying so hard not to be entranced by his dark chocolate skin.

"The stuff in your cart looks like you are preparing a large meal or either shopping for two weeks."

"No," she smiled nervously. "Every Saturday I have a dinner at my home for women of domestic abuse. We sit and talk and we try to help them see how to get control of their lives and put the situation behind them."

"Wow," he said looking perplexed. "Are you a psychologist or counselor?"

"No. I, I was in an abusive relationship. Actually, I was married to the fool." There, she had said it. It felt like a never ending barrage of bricks had been lifted off of her. She had come full circle. Inside, she smiled harder. She tried to conceal it from this handsome stranger but It could not be contained.

"Why the big grin?"

"I've really never told a *stranger* that until after I've known them for a while, unless they are a woman of course."

"Well, first of all, my name is Robert, so now I'm not a stranger and second of all, I am very happy for you. It seems as if you have come a long way, you know, leaving him and now helping these other women."

"Well my name is Jasmine, and I am planning on opening a help Center one day or at least maybe having more meetings during the week, you know. But for now I'm doing what I can for them and for me of course. I'm still working on me, getting my life back into a positive one. Finding out the things that I like and what makes me happy." Drifting for a moment, she remembered her secret passion for photography which had been restrained throughout most of her life. She had married young and her dreams had been forced to be nonexistent next to his.

"Well from your laughter it seems like you are certainly on the right path. It's great that you understand getting you together first before you move on to the next relationship in life. So many women *and men* leave relationships and take all their views and outlooks from that relationship into the next and they end up treating the new person the same way as the previous... uh, I'm sorry. I'm preaching."

She wanted to laugh. *If only he knew*. "Well," she hesitated, "When I first got divorced I did try to go date and jump into relationships and I was just like you said. But I learned. We all have to learn some things the hard way. But it's been just me and my kids for a while now." Thoughts of Tremaine and the others circled to the front of her head as the lie left her lips, but she quickly vowed not to let those fools ruin this moment. "Counseling and talking to other experienced people has been a big help. I'm not trying to date right now *but* I'm not turning down the opportunity to meet new friends either!"

He laughed. "So are you saying you would like to get to know me as a friend?"

"Yes," she smirked.

"I would like that too." He took out a pen and small piece of paper from his pocket. He wrote down his number and his name on one side, turned it over and wrote a long paragraph, it seemed, folded it and handed it to her. "Well, Jasmine, It was nice to meet you. Please, call me. I am looking forward to knowing the thoughts behind those beautiful eyes. See you."

"Bye. Nice to meet you too," she said as he walked away. Her eyes glued to his athletic silhouette, she watched with enjoyment until his slightly bow legged stride had turned the corner and disappeared. She quickly unfolded the note he had given her, and silently read the words that seemed to be meant just for her. It was everything she had tried to do and all that she had imagined herself becoming. And it was so enchanting that a total stranger had walked into her life and written down words she needed to hear every day, forever:
 Jasmine,

 "Unless constructive –selfish, like Arctic Owl, athlete-pilot-beaver-bee, I train first me, what can save or respect me? Absolute nothing. Each swallow works hard to be perfect pilot-provider-builder-trainer-teacher-lover-mate…So, each day like a bird, perfect thyself first!" –Dr. Emanuel Bronner
 Robert

There were tears welling in her eyes. There was a smile pressed beneath their path.

"Now you are crying?" came the voice of the elderly woman who had returned down the aisle. "Let me guess, you are crying cause you are happy to be alive, right?"

"Uh huh," Jasmine nodded.

"Yeah right, I saw that tall hunk talking to you, that's why you don't know whether to smile or cry!"

They both chuckled.

Wow, she thought. *He was really nice.*

* * * *

It had been two weeks since Jasmine had heard anything from Tremaine. Her calls had gone straight to voicemail, her messages never returned, and her texts never answered. She had wished so hard that he was different.

Almost deep into her depression she was rescued by the huge grin pressed between the puffy cheeks of four year old Malcolm, running into the kitchen, "Look momma! Look at Kiara!"

Lumbering behind him, Kiara, wearing the oversized high heeled shoes of her mother with Jasmine's purse weighing down her bright skinned shoulder, smiled up at Jasmine. Jasmine laughed, bending down and wrangling both children tightly in her arms. Following a mushing kiss to both of their faces she giggled, "I love you both so very, very much! So much!" While squeezing them both and shaking them tenderly, the folded note from Robert fell from her purse.

Robert. She had almost forgotten.

After dinner, with the children drifting off to sleep in their beds, Jasmine sat quietly sipping green tea. The hand written note, flipping and twirling between her fingers would not let go of her attention. The longer she stared the easier to remember the number became. *He was hot.* She wanted so desperately to call. The kids were sleeping and her sister would be off from work, walking through the door soon. *Call him,* she thought, "No. I'm just lonely," she reasoned. "But I wonder what he can do." Jasmine guzzled a huge swallow of searing tea without a flinch. It was nothing compared to her own rising temperature. *You're just horny! Don't do it! Don't you dare call.*

"Seven, seven, zero..." her fingers seemed to dial by themselves. As soon as the ringing began, her heart started to break through her chest.

"Hello?" his deep, seductive, yet trust imparting voice answered.

"Hi, can I speak to-o-o-o Robert?"

"Well, Hi. Jasmine, right?" His tone changed to a mellow innocence.

"Yeah, you remembered my, my voice?"

"Of course. How could I forget you? I was beginning to think that you weren't going to call."

"Oh, well you know, work, the kids," she stumbled. "So-o-o-o what's up for tonight?"

Her heart pounded, each beat almost audible during the lengthy pause.

"Nothing much," he firmly broke the silence. "Pretty much winding down. It's been a long day, a good day though."

Jasmine's courage was now hotter than the tea cup, with her butterflies now slain and melting. "Well," she spoke in her sexy voice, "why don't you come over and we can wind down together?"

Robert chuckled lightly, "Uh that might not be a good idea."

"Why not?"

"We barely know each other. And you have children. Wouldn't want them to see a strange man in the house late at night."

The shock quickly chilled Jasmine's burning heat. She had never been turned down like that. "Ok... Well, maybe tomorrow?" she recovered.

"Or maybe we could go out somewhere," he suggested.

What? Is he gay? She thought. "Uh, Robert, how old are you?"

"I'm twenty-eight."

"Hmmm," she wondered aloud.

"What's wrong? Too old for you?"

"No, no, I'm twenty-four. It just seems that you are a very nice guy, too nice."

He sighed. "Just being me, respectful. If you prefer a thug or disrespect, then don't let me waste your time."

"Oo-oo-oo! Alright now! That's a little hard of a comeback for a nice boy," Jasmine teased.

"Just take time to get to know me. I'm thuggish in protecting the people in my life not thuggish against them."

A pleasant feeling emerged as she curled up in the faux leather recliner. He was different, far different than any guy she had talked to. Nice guys were definitely never in season for her. But he was so hot. He had her attention.

* * * *

On Sunday, the inconsistent chill of November in Georgia was warmed by her anticipation of seeing Robert again. Jasmine cocked a smile and winked at herself in front of the mirror. *Bet he won't say no to this,* she smirked. Tight DK jeans hugged her thick legs and cupped her gun holster thighs. A new pink turtle-neck sweater lined her slim upper body, with her breast pushed up high and proud underneath. The finishing touch was a pair of wedge heeled, pink, knock off Manolo boots. With hair done and a fresh manicure she felt so sexy. *But what clubs are worth goin to or even open on a Sunday?* She questioned. *Or maybe we're just chillin at his home. Wonder if he's married or something. Dang girl! I forgot to even ask.*

Robert had asked her to meet him at the Barnes and Noble at Southlake. She was slightly annoyed that he did not pick her up from her apartment, yet as before she was greatly attracted and still intrigued. She arrived finding him standing against his black Jeep, his white smile brighter than the two o'clock sky above them. With his black jeans draped over his tan Timbs, a long sleeve matching shirt with black print design, he looked perfect as she walked up to him. Her five foot, six frame perched upon four inch wedges brought her widened brown eyes closer to his but she still looked up to his six foot waved and neatly trimmed head.

She answered his hello with a hug, squeezing her body into his.

"Hello yourself," she then replied. "So, where are we goin?"

"We're here," he said, still smiling.

"What? We're goin to the book store?"

"Just for a minute," he sensed her agitation. "Then we will go. Don't worry, you'll like it. Just give this 'nice boy' some of your time."

She wanted to scream and curse but she was already there with him, and he was looking too good to let him go.

With her hand in his, he led her in, not to the coffee area, not to the magazines, but straight to the children's section. For nearly fifteen minutes she listened and watched as he read children's stories to a filled section of bright eyed and imagination filled children. His facial expression and changing tones excited not only them but also easily brought a smile to Jasmine's face.

After the book store, they ate at Charley's down the street. The conversation with Robert was refreshing. They talked about future goals and their present lives. His empathy with her helping abused women made her swoon. She even shared her passion for photography which she had never felt comfortable sharing with anyone before. There was so much freedom, talking with him. Later, they found themselves at the movies watching *The World is Not Enough*. Every so often Jasmine would look over at his handsome face, which appeared to be glued to the screen. On more than one occasion she crossed her legs, perching one leg atop of the other knee, bouncing her ankle, making sure the bright pink Manolo knock off caught whatever small amount of light in the theater and sparkled just enough to make him look. She smirked as he tried to hide his eyes which cut glances to her foot wear and thighs from time to time. *He is a nice man*, she gambled. *But he is still a man!* Her confidence assured she was in control. That night, he was going to be hers.

The hard slam of the front door eclipsed the laughter coming from the television. Alicia cocked her brow, gave Jasmine a bewildered look, then turned toward the clock on the opposite wall.

"You home already?"

"Shut up," Jasmine barked, stomping past Alicia to plop down in the recliner. Her manicured fingertips pulled and stretched off the pink knock off boots, adding fuel to her frustration with each tug.

"Ummm, bad date?" Alicia tried once more.

"Let me tell you!" Jasmine broke rapidly. "This idiot spent half the day with me, bought me coffee, dinner, took me to the movies and book store. Hmph, he gave me great conversation and was checking me out from head to feet on the sly all night. Then, we went to his place. He said he wanted to give me this book that he thought I would enjoy reading. I'm thinking it's a nice boy line to get me there so I play along, thinking 'it's about to go down,' and this sucka shows me his very nice apartment, gives me the book and takes me back to my car!"

Alicia said nothing. With a brow still cocked, followed by a half roll of her eyes, she stared at her sister as Jasmine sat hunched down in the recliner, grinding her teeth and breathing rapidly.

"So-o-o-o-o," Alicia teased once more, "On your *first* date, he took you out, paid for everything, you had great conversation, he showed you his place, which I'm assuming he didn't have a wife, and then, on your *first* date, he DOESN'T try to screw you before the night ends, and you have a problem with this?"

Jasmine grinded her teeth and pressed her lips even tighter as Alicia's sarcastic grin could not keep itself from forming in front of her.

"Alicia, you are too young. I don't know why I even bothered," she reasoned. "You wouldn't understand. I'm not even going to try and explain."

"Ahem," Alicia cleared her throat, still grinning. "It would be sad, yet entertaining to hear you try."

"Shut up Alicia! Just shut up."

* * * *

The earth is a constant sphere which revolves in a never-ending spin. The sun seems to rise in the east and set in the west. Mother Nature reveals her splendor in the spring and shows her variegation in the fall. The rain falls to the earth and evaporates to fill the clouds just so it can fall again. It has been this way and forever will be.

It was the month of June, 2001, as Jasmine drove on the expressway towards home. She had just delivered the pictures for her first major photo shoot. She had been hired to take pictures at a Silver Sixties party for some upper class club in the Buck-Head community. As one hand held the steering wheel the other hand held the check up in front of the smile branded upon her face. *I am great*, she thought. *I am finally doing this!* She thought about how nervous she had been, fumbling with her equipment and worrying about the lighting. She remembered how she almost canceled. She worried that all those *snooty folks* might notice that her equipment was not as professional as she would have liked. With the support of her family and friends she had gone anyway, and had taken the most perfect pictures. She was beginning her dream, and she had family to share it with.

Family, she thought. *Kiara has just turned four and Malcolm will be six in two months. My babies are growing so fast.* As she thought of them, thoughts of the children's father came to her mind. She had gone through so much, though she had come so far. She was like steel now. Yet, at the same time she had learned to be as the bark on pine trees, holding firm enough to protect yet not too hard to peel away to show the heart of the tree. She had learned to trust. And she had learned with no better friend than the one who had walked into her life almost two years ago. Robert, had become her best friend. He had proved loyal and lasting. When the sun was shining he had been there, and he had pulled up the water boots and slipped on the rain jacket when the storms of life had rampaged through. With him there was no wife, no 'soon to be divorced', no others, no hidden past. With him, it was weeks not days before he had entered her home. They would meet out at places like the park, the movies, or the mall. And he still remained. Many times before, Jasmine had longed for people to be forgiving of her and accepting, and he had been the only one to fulfill her dream. Robert had witnessed her worst, but he always found understanding. And when she wanted him to share the good times he had always been there. He had been there for transmissions and changing tires, through lost jobs and burglaries. When everything she had ever wanted was someone simply needing her in their life, and he had never been too proud to shout how greatly he did. When she had closed her eyes every night, her last sight had been the many stuffed animals, balloons, and the silk rose singles clasped with tiny white bears which adorned every corner of her bedroom. Each had been a gift from him on some not necessarily special occasion. Though, as he had said 'each occasion with her was special.'

Jasmine was in tears as she pulled into her complex. Through the wells in her eyes she squinted at the check once more, and smiled at the diamond ring snugly clasped around her finger. A ring whose provider still awaited an answer. He had helped her build the little dark room in her hall closet. She had developed her first pictures there, at home. She had started her business with help from this best friend.

It's been three years since my ex-husband, she thought. *Maybe it's time now. Maybe not.* She wiped her tears from her face as she walked towards the door. "I just don't want to make another mistake," she reasoned aloud, staring at the diamond once more. *I just don't know. I just wish God would tell me what to do.* "What do I do?"

Sometimes, in this crazy experience called life, the very things we ask for we do not see when they are given. Sometimes, we search so desperately for perfection we forget we live in an imperfect world. And sometimes, many times, we get accustomed to the way things have always been and seem to always be. Yes, the earth will always revolve in a never-ending spin, but each time it comes round we don't have to look at the sun from the same view. For we might just see that it does not rise in the east and set in the west but it is the sphere of earth that sets around the sun. And even though Mother Nature will always bloom in the spring and begin a color filled nap in fall, no one ever said we had to come inside and forget about her when she is sleeping in winter, because winter isn't when she's sleeping at all. That is when she has the grill fired up high, cooking up spring's new batch. Even the unbreakable cycle of water shows more than its fall and rise. We still drink it, we bath in it, we defile it, we lose it, we learn from it, but it continues on its course. It is we who have the choice to see the differences on the same circle of life. It is we who possess the very thing we often ask from a higher power –that which we were already given: free will.

As Jasmine opened her front door, she smiled at her difference, there before her. Then she darted quickly and quietly up the stairs to grab her small camera. She returned to the living room, aimed, and snapped a picture of her difference. "Out of the mouths of babes," she whispered, staring at the answer to her question. An irrepressible smile showed on her face, a smile that had grown ten times its size since two years ago.

It was Saturday. The children and Robert had prepared the meal and snacks for her women's help group. Now exhausted and sleeping upon the living room floor in front of the television was Robert, with Malcolm nudged near his side and Kiara napping on his chest. Her little arms were wrapped around the only true father she had known, with her hands gently clasped behind the neck of someone who had always been there, and who would always remain.

The Beginning…

"Without the seasoning, an eighty dollar meal in a five star restaurant is the same as a ten dollar steak in a neighborhood diner."

Regrets of Indulgence
(Taste)

I hate my grandfather. Look at him, lying there in that coffin, all shriveled and bald. To embalm him, I know they had to drain out more alcohol than blood. He was a waste of human flesh. Of course, I can't say that with my grandmother sitting here. Not that anything anyone says could ever weaken her. She's too strong. I, I guess I'll just be respectful to her... of him... for her.

I love my grandmother. I paid for everything. I paid for the casket. It's the best; top of the line. But I did it for my grandmother, not for him. My grandmother has always been there for me. My grandfather dying was like a fly landing on my plate and I flick it off, clean away the food it landed on, and keep eating, never thinking about it again. But if something happened to my grandmother, I'd lose it. Everything I know would fall apart.

So there I was, at the wake for my sorry grandfather, finally.

"Julian? Julian Cotero? Is that you?" some strange lady said, staring at me. "Why the last time I saw you, you was just a little bitty boy! Now look at you! All growed up and handsome! Etna, Etna?"

"What girl?" another elderly lady answered. "What you callin me for?"

"Look here! This is Julian all grown. Ain't he handsome and nice looking?"

"Oh yes, yes! Ida Mae, is this your grand boy, all grown and nice looking?"

"Yes, this is Julian," my grandmother smiled.

"I heard you a big time record producer, up there with that, that umm, P-dragon," the first lady chimed in. "Making all that music for these young folk today. You know I listen to some of that hippy hop myself. Your Auntie might be old but I can get my groove on now!"

"Barb!" Etna laughed, gesturing for her to stop.

"I'm sorry son," Barb said, now in a calmer tone. "I know you must miss your granddad. I know he meant a lot to you. Y'all call your Auntie for whatever you need. Alright?"

Out of respect for my grandmother, I could only smile. I can deal with ignorant, illiterate, second uncles and third aunts coming up and claiming to know me. But where on earth did they come off claiming that I missed that loser?

It was that way for the rest of the evening. I saw aunts, uncles, cousins, great aunts, third cousins, and cousins by mouth, coming up telling me and my grandmother how sorry they were for our loss. Loss? I know I had to be nice out of respect for my grandmother but it was pretty hard. My 'dear' old grandfather was never there for me as a grandfather or a father figure. I was told he worked a lot but from what I always saw he just drank a lot. My grandmother was my mother, father, grandmother, and grandfather. As far as I'm concerned my grandfather served no purpose in my life.

The wake was scheduled to end around eight. There were still a lot of people hanging around and talking. My little sister, Tiana, and her boyfriend said their 'fair well' to everyone. T hugged us and told us she'd see us back at the house. T and I have always been close. She's four years younger than me. She and my grandmother are the only family I've ever known… really known. In the music industry, which is my life, you meet friends, some true, some are like glass and break under the slightest pressure. And of course you have the really fake friends, the ones who are all about the money and the notoriety. That's why Tiana, handles everything in my company. She's my V.P., my manager, my executive coordinator, my 'take care of everything' person. What I miss, she catches. What gets screwed up when I'm not there, she puts back together and makes sure it doesn't happen again. If something ever happened to T, I would sell the company or shut it down. No one could ever replace her.

When Tiana and her man walked out of the funeral home doors, a cool breeze rushed in. It felt a little too cool to be the middle of summer. Before the door could close behind them, a short old man, brown skin, wrinkled face with dark glasses, a fedora, and a dark zoot suit that looked like it was from the gangsters of Harlem during the 1940's, walked in. Now I'm six feet, two hundred twenty pounds, very much in shape, chiseled beautiful skin, and from a teenager until now I have never been afraid of anything or anyone. But this stranger just gave me an uneasy feeling.

He walked slowly over to the casket, seeming to hesitate with each step. When I think about it, he had my grandfather's swagger; the way he would lean, as if he were about to fall over if he didn't hurry up and make it to a seat. The man put both hands on the casket rim and stared down at my grandfather as he shook his head. "Mr. Bit, Mr. Bit," he said, still shaking his head.

'Mr. Bit' or 'Bit Cotero' was my grandfather's nickname. I never knew why people called him that. I assumed it was some part of the old southern black culture, which I prided myself on leaving behind when I went to college. I left the ghetto mindset and speech also. I was always better than that. I used to joke to myself that maybe because he was known to drink a 'bit' too much. I don't know. In my childhood I spent a lot of time amusing myself. At my wake and my funeral I want people to crack jokes and enjoy themselves, not sit around sad or uptight.

Anyway, after staring down at my grandfather, the old man made a bee line for me and my grandmother. That uneasy chill grew stronger, and my Armani shirt and tie seemed to be a little tighter.

"Hello, Julian," the old man greeted. The way he said it was as if I actually knew him. I mean, there were lots of people coming up to me that night, talking to me like they knew me because they *had* known me when I was a child. But when this old man spoke to me, it was like, like I knew him.

"Hello, how are you?" I hesitated.

"Wonderful, wonderful," he smiled, his eyes barely visible through his dark glasses. "Well, you have truly grown haven't you? Tall, good looking, and very gifted I've heard. You probably don't know me but I've known you since you were born. Oh how gifted and blessed you are! Just wonderful, wonderful!"

I don't trust anyone in this world. I believe only what I see with my own eyes or find out with my own research. I grew up teaching myself that people in this world are never trustworthy. I don't know what it was, but with every word this old man spoke, I felt as if I had known him all my life, as if I could about believe anything he was saying.

"I've watched your career," he continued. "Not just since the first song you produced but even since your days in the band in middle school. You were exceptional then and extraordinary now."

Okay, right then, the chill and strange feelings I had felt, disappeared. Now, I felt this old man was either a stalker or some pedophile that had molested me and I had suppressed the memory somehow. Maybe that sounds bad, but I have never known anyone, black or white, that had good intentions toward me or my career unless it brought financial gain or status for themselves. I wanted to grab him by his collar and ask 'who are you?' but at that same moment my grandmother, who had taken my hand a moment earlier squeezed it tightly as if she was reading my mind.

"So you came to pay your respects to your mentor?" he smiled.

My 'mentor'? Is this old man smoking crack?

"You must be so thankful to have had him in your life, Julian. You must be so thankful that he shared his gift with you. You have been just like a mirror reflecting Mr. Bit's light into the hearts of this dark, dark world! It's wonderful, just wonderful!"

Okay, he was either senile or had my family confused with someone else. Yeah, I probably have touched the lives of people everywhere. I've produced hit songs for artist in every genre of music. I've traveled all over the world; I'm well known and highly respected all over the world. Shoot! People have come up to me and said they've made babies to my music! Yeah, I am all that and more. But this strange old man was crazy to think that David "Bit" Cotero had one ounce of contribution to my talent or my success! Let me tell you what Bit Cotero did for me...

When I was one, my mother and I moved to Griffin, Georgia to live with my grandparents. We moved in with my dad's parents because my mother's parents were already deceased and she had never been close to any of her other relatives who all lived out west. And my father? Well, when we were moving into Bit Cotero's house he was moving into the state penitentiary.

See, my story is kind of rough, but it's a need to know...for me. And if you don't care to hear it, here it is anyway.

I was born February 7, 1972. My dad named me Julian, after the great Jazz saxophonist Julian Cannonball Adderley. My dad was in a Jazz band and doing pretty well, supporting me and my mother. But when finances got a little tight he began doing part-time odd jobs for people, like cleaning out junk and trash, cutting grass, and so on. That was going good too, until the one job he got, doing work for some lady. Long story short, he said he didn't, she said he raped her. I was too young to know what went on but when I got older, people told me he was convicted with practically no evidence and basically the woman's word. Being that it was before DNA testing and we were in the south, I believe it.

My dad was sentenced to 22 years in prison. I had just turned one year old. Six years later, the lady became terminally ill with some disease and on her death bed confesses that he never touched her. So he gets out. By then my mother has moved on with her life. Sure, she kept in touch through letters and pictures, making sure he had some kind of relationship with me. But as far as their relationship, that was over. She had met a new man, remarried, and now I had a little sister. That was too much for my father to take when he returned. He lost six years of his life to 'the system', his family to a lie, and he lost the love of his life.

My father convinced my mom to meet him at my grandparent's house just to talk, to say the things he needed to say. They went to the back room of the house to talk in private. No one knows what was said. No one knows what was in their hearts. On that day, in that room, my father shot and killed my mother, then shot and killed himself.

I was in first grade. I remembered being so pissed off because it was time for recess when my grandfather came to check me out of school early. The only other thing I remember is my little sister crying, letting only me hold her, and me asking all day, 'Where is my momma?'

And that's how we came to live in my grandparent's house for the second time, though, this time it was to be my permanent home. Tiana's father was career military. Of course being active duty overseas, he had to sign over custody to the nearest relative and not wanting to split us apart he let Tiana remain with me and my grandparents, who loved her like their own blood. The first year there, I never wanted to leave the house again. That was the beginning of my dislike for my grandfather. That year he had to beat me to make me go to school. He had no compassion for a grieving little boy about to be seven years old. Everything was just 'be a man' and 'be tough' and 'go on with life' crap. I wanted to ignore everyone and everything but of course he beat me for not speaking when spoken to and for being impolite to people.

Being so introverted, away from friends and family and always in my own misery, I quickly found a love for music. Just the right song could always be an escape or an answer to some problem. I imagined that to create my own 'ladders' or 'stairways' to escape or find answers would be perfect. I begged my grandfather over and over for an electric guitar. His answer was that I only needed to concentrate on my grades in school. With his tightwad, selfish self, it was always only the basic necessities. My begging for the electric guitar was relentless. For an eight to nine year old I was full of passion for something that seemed unreachable.

A few months after my ninth birthday, at the beginning of summer, I came home on the last day of school to find my grandmother greeting me at the front door with the biggest grin.

"You've got a surprise lying on your bed."

"What is it?" I remember lighting up.

"Just go see!"

I ran down the hall, dropping my backpack halfway there and found a large gift wrapped rectangular box on my bed. As I tore back the wrapping paper the last letters in the word *Guitar*, caught my eye, but before I could finish imagining myself playing along with the endless Jazz and R&B tapes left to me from my father's belongings, my heart dropped back down just as quickly as it had been lifted. It was a brand new, glossy, beautiful, ACOUSTIC guitar. I was so mad and sad at the same time. I stormed to the kitchen and laid the reclosed box, with guitar inside, and wrapping paper beside the trash. When asked 'why' by my grandmother, with eyes full of tears I said, "I wanted an electric guitar! E-L-E-C-T-R-I-C!" My grandmother just looked at me with that look that has always been more powerful than any beat down. I saw she felt my pain but I could also see her disappointment in me. To this day I have felt and still feel so bad for what I did. But of course, before I could ever overcome my spoiled nine year old pride and apologize on my own, my grandfather reintroduced my butt to his thick country leather belt. He told me that I would learn to play *that* guitar and that I would play it every day of the summer and that I was an ungrateful spoiled child. *Why did he care?* I remembered thinking. My grandmother had saved every day, cleaning people's homes for little to nothing, and bought me that guitar. He never even wanted me to have it! So what did he care?

It's funny, my grandfather didn't want me to have a guitar. He didn't want me to have anything, I guessed. But when I got one he made me play every day. Maybe he thought I would hate it so much that I would give it up. But I learned how to play an ACOUSTIC guitar. And then I learned to play the piano, the saxophone, viola, and drums.

Though he never took time to tell me I was good or come to my shows given by the band I put together in high school, he did find time to drink and work all the time. He never had time for me. Throughout all of my school years, he never came to anything. It was only my grandmother. He always had to work all night, and on the weekends he had his two-day hangovers from drinking all week and didn't want to do anything else unless it was whipping my butt. I'll admit, I can remember two times, and only two, that he tried to talk to me about my music. Both times he was half drunk and I was running late for a performance. At that time and even now nothing was important enough to deter me from my musical aspirations. I just told him we would talk later. But of course, when he was sober he never said anything to me or had forgotten about it so I never said anything to him. I figured that when he was drinking he just got mellow and probably wanted to make up for not being there for me. But what could he ever tell me about music? My memories of my grandfather are of him always working or being drunk three hundred and sixty days out of the year. What could he possibly ever tell me?...

Staring at that old man with the dark glasses, I couldn't help wanting to choke him. Who was he to think my grandfather was a mentor to me or that I was thankful for having him in my life? If my grandmother wasn't there I would have put him in the casket with my grandfather and have it buried that night. But she was there. So I couldn't disrespect her.

"Yeah," I said, "I'm thankful." *Thankful that he was no longer here so maybe I could remember less of him not being there for me.*

"Good, good!" he smiled. "Well you take care of your grandmother now. Ya gotta spend more time at home if you wanna get more success away."

"What?" I frowned. What the heck did that mean?

"Take care…," he smiled. As he turned to walk away, he began singing some song, something about making it to the top but not having anything, or something like that.

A little too late, I thought. *He should have told my work-alcoholic grandfather that, years ago.*

"…That's what Mr. Bit used to say!" he yelled when he turned around at the door and looked at me.

"What the …," I caught myself. "Grandma, who in the world was that?"

"Who?" she said staring up at me from her chair.

"That old man, with the dark glasses that just left."

"What old man?"

"Never mind grandma, never mind." It was late and she must have been too tired and dozing in and out of sleep the whole evening as she sat there, trying to show a smile for people who came to say hello.

On the way home, I thought of all the people I had seen at the wake. Some, I hadn't seen since high school. Some, I didn't really know but they all knew me. More than likely it was my entertainment fame and money they knew. Shoot, most of my classmates never really knew me. They wasted their time going out, hanging out, and dreaming. But those mofos used to dance to music I made for concerts and shows I promoted. When I was seventeen, I had mastered music on a higher level than anyone my age. I soon began learning the business behind the music. Since my first year in college, I've produced more songs than they could ever remember the words to. They wasted their time with their pants sagging, no drive having, all talk and dream flashing, fast running athletic but can't read, good for nothing except end user bottom of the food chain and struggling, more money around the neck wearing, zero cash in the bank non investing, 'shawty' hollering player pretending, fake hair wearing ashamed to be natural, nappy head bobbing, fake eyelash batting, acrylic nail investing, three hours on the weave but zero minutes in the gym slacking, 'can't wet my hair' complaining, got their own house and car ranting but can't afford to get the grass cut hassling, yet still looking for a man to provide playing, fraternity and sorority pledging cause they can't be a part of reality missing, sexing as the ultimate thrill seeking, and all of them trying to be a celebrity. They were millions of mindless sheep that made me rich. While they were dreaming, I was building reality. I have been and always will be better than them. It tickled me. The ones I grew up around, who were around my same age, now had kids, baby daddies, baby mommas, little or no money, no property but plenty of car rims stacked on the back porch. Like Andre, my semi best friend in high school. He had lived three houses down from me. He was naturally gifted in learning any instrument. I tried and tried to get him to push himself and work hard like me. But Andre was a lady's man, a pretty boy. When I wanted to create and have all night writing sessions on the weekends he wanted to go out and chase women, or go out to the movies, ball games, and other time wasters. It's sad. He could have been with me at the top of the world and had any women he wanted, but he was still living here, in this town, married to the same girl he fell for in high school. He still lived in the house he grew up in, passed on to him by his parents, with three kids and a nine to five as a grocery store manager. The last time I saw Andre, he was at a park running after two of his kids while his wife sat on a bench holding the baby. He pretended to be so happy when I saw him. I know it wasn't real. How could it be? A wife, three kids, a regular job, and still living in the same little house, come on! He said he would pull out his sax and play every now and then for his family. It probably was a way for him to escape his misery and dream about what he could have had. But Andre didn't want to do the work to be better than average. I worked hard and still do. I could buy just about anything or travel anywhere I wanted to. I sent my grandparents new furniture and new everything. They would have had a big new house but they, more so my grandfather, just wanted to stay there.

Driving down the road I thought of how I hadn't been to the house in years. T brought grandma, I mean my grandmother, to the wake and I'd met them there. Even in the dark, the street looked different. Even my grandmother looked much older than she did the last time I saw her face to face. Her hair was silver now, with more wrinkles on her face. Her eyes were worn and sunken and she was much thinner than before. Had I been away that long?

The house seemed so different to me. All the furniture and appliances were new; things I paid for but had never seen. The only thing that remained the same was my old room. The last time I'd been here was in my second year of college. I didn't even come here when T graduated high school. I'd flown in, gone straight to the auditorium, and afterwards I went straight to the airport. I guess I have always been very busy. But my grandmother had everything. I made sure of that. And T was always flying in to represent both of us at holidays and family gatherings. The more I walked around the house, the more alien it seemed to me.

I stepped in the doorway of my grandmother's room. She was sitting half-awake in her leather rocker.

"Julian, are you staying here tonight?" she said so softly.

"Yes, grandma. I'll be here for a while."

"What's 'a while'? One day, Two days?" she teased, trying to show a smile.

"No," I smiled back. "I'll be here for a while, until I know you're going to be okay. I know I've been away so long and never visit much… but I call you every day."

"Yes you do call," She arched one brow, "But not every day, MISTER! Some things can't be learned over the phone."

"Grandma!" I whined. I felt like I was twelve again. "I try calling every day. It is in my heart's plan to. But anyway, what else do I need to *learn*? Like Aunt Barbara said, I'm 'the big time record producer.' I don't need anything." My grandmother just smiled at me and rocked. She and I had always been silly with one another. Although, the truth of it was, I *didn't* need anything. "Grandma, do you know where my guitar is? The white one, the first one. I didn't see it in my room."

"White guitar... Guitar, guitar?" she thought aloud. "You mean that beautiful guitar your granddaddy bought for you? I remember the day we gave it to you, 'E-L-E-C-T-R-I-C.' I remember how upset you were," she chuckled.

I was so embarrassed. "Grandma, I'm so sorry for that. But what do you mean *he* bought it for me?"

"Well, goodness child! You didn't think I bought it with the little money I made from cleaning, did you?"

"Well, yes." I said, feeling a little stupid.

"Boy, your granddaddy bought that guitar."

"But *you* gave it to me?" Saying that to her, somehow made me believe that my version of the past would prevail as the true one.

"Julian, I may be older now but I remember saying 'you have a surprise in your room.' I would never say I bought something if I didn't."

That was true. My grandmother would never lie to me. *But why would my grandfather have bought it for me if he didn't want me to have it?*

"I think it's in the attic."

"The attic?"

"Your granddaddy must have forgotten to bring it back down with all of your other things after we had your room painted."

"Why did you have my room painted?"

"It had to be painted after we had the ceiling and sheetrock repaired"

"What repairs? Why?"

"From the fire, boy!" she grunted.

"What fire?!"

"The new stove you bought had a recall on it; it was defective. It caught fire but it was small. It was only the wall between the kitchen and your room. But we had all the information and warranties in the paperwork that came with it and the company took care of all the repairs."

"Why didn't anyone tell me?" I scratched my head.

"Well, we thought you'd find out when you came home that Thanksgiving but you ended up in Europe with that girl band you promoted that year. Then it all got repaired and we just didn't want to bother you on your tour and all."

I felt so distant. "Grandma, I'm sorry."

"That's alright boy. You're home now. If you go up in the attic to get your guitar, could you get that framed magazine cover you sent me too? The one with you on Rocking Stone?"

"You mean, Rolling Stone?"

"Yeah, baby, that's it."

"Grandma, why do you have that in the attic? I thought you loved that cover?"

"I do. But after we got it back, I just felt it was safer to keep it in the attic."

"Back? Back from where?"

"The police evidence lockup."

I sighed. I thought back to my meditation exercises. "Okay. Why was that framed cover, of me on Rolling Stone, in the police evidence?"

"Because of the robbery, boy! You have been away too long!"

"Y'all were robbed! When? What happened?"

"It was nothing. Some hoodlums that you went to high school with are now too grown and out on the street, up to no good, and they thought that since we are your grandparents we might have some money stashed here in the house. Your granddaddy convinced them that we didn't have anything so they left. But that one, the one with the gun, he had to get something. So he took your framed cover, I heard him tell the other one that it was worth some money. But the police caught them running down the street. So later, after everything, we got the frame back."

"This is crazy! How could no one have told me this?" I grunted.

"Well, we did try telling you about the robbery. Your granddaddy tried calling you. That was when I was sick and he said he kept leaving messages with your secretary. She said she did tell you that your granddaddy was calling. I guess that heffa was lying!"

I wanted to crawl deep into a dark hidden place. I could never let my grandmother know that my secretary *did* give me the messages but I had always been too busy to call my grandfather back. I just knew he wanted to talk about one of his business ideas again or wanted to give me drunken advice about my music. I just didn't have time for that nonsense. Instead of just saying that he called, he should have told her what it was about. It was his fault!

The rungs to the pull down stair case leading into the attic squeaked with each step I took. As I yanked on the beaded pull string, clicking power to the lights in the attic, I was immediately a child again. So many things from my past packed away in boxes or piled up here and there. So many images of my years of seven to twelve, like one of the times when my grandfather was doing some work in the attic and he left the stairs down. Tiana was four at the time. She disappeared and we all searched for an hour or so, everywhere in the house, outside, at the neighbor's, and in the woods across the street. Finally, my grandmother was walking past the pull-down stairs when she heard a faint voice from the attic saying, "Help me, git down, help me gamma." T had decided to climb up after my grandfather had come down. I guess after exploring for a while she returned to find that she wasn't quite coordinated enough or tall enough to climb back down on steps that steep. We all had a good laugh.

There were other times involving the attic, like exploring or pretending with my imaginary friends, when my grandfather wasn't home of course. There were so many boxes and old trunks of things that belonged to my uncles and aunts… and to my dad. How I missed my dad and my mom. I had missed them every day of my life. Every time the bad thoughts or the sadness would come I'd just work on my music. Creating a song or composing a beat would erase the pain. Music, had been my psychologist, my friend, my lover, my birth, and will be my end. Mastering the cords to breathe life into soundless thoughts to morph into art had been my rite of passage. Music had made me a man.

I straddled the rafters and stepped on and off the few boards scattered throughout the attic. There were two lights in the attic that lit up most of the space. In the shadow of other neatly stacked boxes lay my first guitar, acoustic, wrapped in plastic. It brought a smile to my face. And right beside it, on top of a small cardboard file box was my framed cover. As I bent down and picked up my frame, the words labeled on the cardboard box caught my eye. *David's Music*. It was old, very old, and sealed with duct tape. *Maybe old albums or forty-fives*, I thought. My grandfather and I had many differences but I loved any type of music and was curious to see what the old man listened to back in his day.

I managed to get the guitar, the framed cover, and the old box down the squeaky attic ladder in two trips.

"Grandma," I said, hauling the box into her room and plopping it down on the floor, "what is this?"

She stopped rocking for a second and slowly cracked open one eye. "That's David's!" she said excitedly, now with both eyes open wide. "Where did you get that?"

"It was in the attic. My frame was on top of it."

She smiled, closed her eyes, and began to rock slowly again. "No surprise he would have put it there with your frame."

"Ma'am?" I questioned. She didn't respond. She just continued to rock, looking half asleep with a smile on her face. "Grandma, what is in here? Can I open it? Are there old records in here?"

"Records?" she stopped rocking, "No child! Just open it and see."

Whatever was in that box that was so special, to make my grandmother smile like that, excited my curiosity. I took my rental car key and tried to rip the old tough duct tape. That didn't work so I got a knife from the kitchen. It was still kind of tough to open but it worked. When I removed the top a stale mildew odor caught my nose.

"Whew!" I gasped.

There were no albums, no records, no eight tracks; only faded paper stacked and packed tightly. I gently pulled a group of papers out of the tight stack. There were musical notes and lyrics on each page. I removed more groups of papers, stacking them on the floor in the same order which they were in the box. There were hundreds of lyrics to songs, all titled by the same author – David Cotero.

"Ok, what is this?" I turned to my grandmother, thinking to myself that this was some joke or had some other ridiculous explanation.

"It's what it says on the box, *David's Music*. It's the music he made"

"Grandma," I said, scratching my head, "Granddaddy couldn't read or write, could he?"

"He could write music in his head, and I wrote down his lyrics and music on paper. That's my handwriting, see? See that there? He'd play it on the piano or a guitar and I learned enough to write down the chords and the lyrics he told me."

I was stunned. *My grandfather played music. My grandfather wrote music. My grandfather wrote music? My grandfather made music! What in the world?!*

"Grandma?" I could only look at her.

My grandmother is not the type to throw something in your face or say I told you so. But she just stopped rocking, opened her eyes fully, and just gave me a soft stare and a gentle grin.

"Grandma?" I asked again. Not really knowing what to ask. So clueless, so suddenly unsure about everything I'd ever known. "How... what... why?"

"Your granddaddy used to be a musician in a band. That's where your father got his music interest from, and you got it from your father."

"But granddaddy hated my music! Why... how could he have ever been in a band? He never listened to mine. He never came to see my shows. How could he have bought that guitar? He hated music! He... that's not..."

"Child, who told you he hated music? Who told you he hated your music?"

No one, I thought to myself. Ashamed at raising my voice to my grandmother, I stared down at the box still half full of songs. Ashamed at my assumption, a lump swelled in my throat.

Once again, slowly rocking in her chair, my grandmother smiled with her eyes closed. "Your granddaddy made you play that acoustic guitar not to punish you, but to make you be the best. You learned the basics, then you were able to create the extraordinary." She stopped rocking, opened her eyes, and stared at me playfully, "You are the best aren't you? Mister big time producer!"

I looked up from my seated position on the floor and couldn't help but smile back at her. But with the smile came the welling of water in my eyes.

"Grandma, did he really like... my music? Did he really listen to it?" It seemed so strange to ask that, to want the opinion, or maybe in a subconscious way, the approval of a man I hated ninety-nine percent of the time.

"Yes boy. He loved your music. The strongest sound in that man's head..." she choked. Then I saw the first tears in her eyes I'd seen in a long time. "…the most terrible sound in that man's head was the sound of those two shots from that day. It drove him crazy, every night, every day. They haunted him. That's when his heavy drinking started. That's when he began working so much. He tried to convince himself that he had to work so much to pay for you to go to college. But when you got that music scholarship, he said he still needed to work as hard because Tiana might want to be a doctor or lawyer. And when she made it into college, he still couldn't stop working so much. The real reason, I know, was that it was his way to make the sounds go away. He tried everything to make those sounds go away, everything. But nothing worked. Nothing, except for one thing." She smiled beneath the tears that had begun to stream. "Whoa child! Every time you played music in this house, he said those awful sounds went away. Every time he played a CD that you produced, the sounds went away. He had every song you ever made on CD, even the ones from those hip hop guys! Lord, where did that music come from? But he had every one. When he heard your music, he was hearing his grandson, his son, and himself. He was hearing his son, alive! For a moment, listening to your music made him forget. You, erased his pain."

There were tears streaming from both of our eyes now. I wasn't quite sure if mine were from my empathy for her or for my newly found loss. I never could have dreamt the things she told me. I never could have written this in my best song composition. But it wasn't fair! He kept to himself, away from me! He was the adult! I was a child!

"Grandma, he never said anything to me! He never tried!"

She stared at me, with a mother's compassion, watching the tears fall down my face. "Julian, he tried," she whispered. "You were just always so mad, mad at everything; mad at the world…"

"He only scolded me! And told me when I was about to do something wrong or…"

"That's not true, Julian. He did try. But you were ready to fight as soon as he looked your way. He wanted to go to your shows but he felt that you didn't want him there. After a while, he didn't know what else to do, what else to try."

"But, but I... He…" I stammered, still searching for a reason to be right, a reason to still hate him. "The only times I remember was when he was drunk and then he wanted to tell me about his dreams and wild ideas."

My grandmother didn't say anything. She just sighed and looked away as she began to rock again. I felt even worse. I was hard and I admit arrogant at times but in this world I had to be, to achieve my goals, my success.

I sifted through the rest of the songs still in the box, skimming the chords and lyrics. Somewhere, almost near the bottom, one of my grandfather's songs hit me like a baseball bat. That's when I understood.

The cliché is, 'you never miss it until it's gone.' Hearing that over and over in our lives is no way as painful as feeling it. That night, in that home, I cried for a man I barely knew. That night, I realized none of my awards, hits, or fame meant anything. My greatest love, which I could mold, shape, and tame to do whatever I wanted, had always been my servant. That night, my greatest love became my teacher. That night, a song molded me. Set to the beats and riffs of a blues melody, the lyrics burned through my soul:

If you climb Mount Everest
and ya momma don't say she's proud,
What you got?
If you please yoself
but you never please one out the crowd,
What you got?
If you taste success
that aint seasoned with the ones you love,
What you got?
Got a million dollar coat

but got a two dollar pair of gloves,
What you got?
What you got?
You got nuttin baby
You aint got nuttin baby

      All my life I thought it had been him. He was the one who had indulged in alcohol and work. I thought somewhere near the end of his life he'd be seeing my success and wishing he'd spent more time with me; wishing he could be a part of my life… but somehow, it turned out to be me who was doing the wishing.

      "Grandma," I could barely say without choking. I felt seven years old again, feeling loss again for the second time in my life. But somehow, it seemed worse than the first, "why didn't anyone ever tell me? How was it that I never knew about all this? How is it that I never know about his music or the way he felt about mine?"

      My grandmother, slowly rocking with closed eyes, gently formed a comforting smile, as if to soften the blow. Then, her rocking slowed to a halt. She opened her eyes, so full of the compassion only a strong mother could have, and she replied, "Boy, you never took time to ask."

"If a blind man grabs a rose by its stem, he would never love a rose."

The Variegated Valley
(Touch)

As Jamal stared into her eyes, a light autumn breeze blew through Casandra's hair, making the curled strands dangle and dance gracefully against her face. With this beautiful sight came the question he had wanted to ask for so long. A question, which was a proclamation, that had been chained by The Voices for so long.

For a moment, he looked out into the valley where the changing of colors marked the changing of season. Multicolored leaves cloaked the entire panorama of trees and covered the hillside where these two sat. The freshly painted white church beamed an effervescent shine enough to hold anyone's attention, yet could not outdo the eminence of the mill which stood opposite the church, across the pond. The mill had a mystic beauty of its own. There was something about the rustic lines in its walls and roof which were illuminated by the sunlight. The faint laughter of Mrs. Ellington's three year old, and the sneeze of Mr. Ellington from the blue house near the pond, melodiously merged with the symphony of blue jays, robins, and warblers chirping throughout the valley. Every now and then, they whisked down to the edge of the pond to search for worms and dead minnows left from little Jonny Simpson's morning fishing trip. The monotony of waves rippling across the pond was being broken by a bass striking near the surface at a low flying dragonfly. The aroma of fried chicken, corn, and broccoli masked the picnic basket between Casandra and Jamal. -A variation of sights, sounds, and scents all merged into the perfect setting; the perfect moment to settle his deliberation and purge his confusion concerning a decision he would soon reveal to her…and to himself.

The two of them had met here in this valley, a valley filled with seasonal changes. Their hearts had grown together within the shadows of the valley's trees which towered like skyscrapers on society's unempathetic streets, and their infallible emotions had lead them here, up on the slopes, to a place where they could look down and see the true beauty of the valley in its entirety.

With her eyes, Cassandra searched the premature lines on his young face, lines which had been made by the power of The Voices. Jamal had always been the talkative one, the conversation starter, and sometimes even too wordy. She never worried about hunting for his thoughts. Her reticence had found a sanctuary in his heart. With the blinking of her eyes, the parting of her lips to reveal a pearly shine, or the simple touch from her hand to his skin he could always discern if she understood his daily poetic utterances of affection. With mostly words he had won her heart, with less than words she had conquered his.

"A penny for your thoughts," she offered. Even with the assured fall atmosphere residing with all Jamal's senses he could still hear and feel the hint of spring whispering from her soothing voice.

He looked deep into her soft brown eyes – eyes which were as mirrors of his own – and with his right hand he gently caressed the side of her face. Then, affectionately, he pushed his fingertips beneath and around her earlobe, where he fondled her ruddy brown hair. Jamal smiled at the woman who sat before him, a woman he had built his whole world around – a construction of blissful diversity which needed only one brick to be made complete.

Jamal gazed out again into the valley. He watched, he listened, and he smelled the harmony of life's diversity that appeared before him. He turned towards Cassandra again. His eyes traveled from her radiant peach skin, to his rugged brown hand, and back towards the valley.

"It'll never work."

"Y'all are from two different backgrounds…different cultures…different…"

"There'll be too many problems."

The voices of society rumbled and roared in his mind as they had since he first kissed her smooth, dark-carnation-colored lips. But now those voices were quieter and although they would never be completely extinguished from the valley, soon, they would retire from his corral of troubles, forever.

His eyes once again resting on her, he answered, "I'm thinking about us."

"What about us?" she asked. As always, her words louder than the voices.

"I want us to be together... permanently... forever."

He said it, something they both felt months before but had concealed their feelings.

As Jamal again looked out upon the interlocking beauty of dappled leaves fluttering and falling in the wind, he knew. As he noticed the equal elegance of the new church and of the old mill, he knew. As he smelled the fetid odor of the pond and the crispy aroma of the picnic basket, he knew. As he heard the variety of birds playing their individual voice-instrumental-songs yet harmoniously sounding as one, he knew. The valley was one. Deep inside he had known all along, about this way of the valley and of the love between Cassandra and he –it was natural.

With a subtle smile, he stared into her eyes, with one hand tightly holding hers, his other hand retrieved a small blue velvet box from his right pocket. Cassandra let out a graceful gasp, her eyes, falling from his, alighting upon the now opened case held in his quivering hand.

"Cassandra Nly Peiser, will you marry me? Will you forever be my heart, which makes me complete; the one who allows me to care for you, letting your every desire become my destined duty?"

The screaming horn from an enraged driver cut off by a taxi pierced the air. Similar horns in the distance and the hustling of hundreds of shoes on the concrete sidewalk beneath Jamal's and Cassandra's feet pounded their eardrums. Careless chatter of passersby and slick words of street vendors filled the area around them.

"What happened?" Cassandra pleaded, her happiness being sucked away by the cars racing by the bus stop bench where these two sat.

"I'm sorry baby," Jamal whispered, searching franticly for his white cane which had fallen, hitting the concrete beneath him. "I heard my stick fall and I let go of your hand."

"It scares me when you do that without warning," she sniffed. "Please baby, grab my hand again. Where are you?" Both of Cassandra's hands reaching in front of her, found his thigh, then began climbing up his torso en route to his arms.

"Here you are sir," a cheerful voice, unknown to either of them offered as its owner placed the white cane in Jamal's hand. "This is so beautiful! Right here, in the middle of downtown!"

"Thank you," Jamal smiled, slipping the strap around his wrist. Then he turned back to Cassandra's voice and captured her searching hands with his.

"Ahhh," she sighed. "I can't stand it when I can't see you! Don't let go of my hand again."

"I won't," he promised, his smile glistening brightly in her eyes with the variegated panorama now reappearing behind him.

There was a glimmer in her tears and a vaunting sparkle in her smile reflecting from the diamond, set upon the ring within the velvet case.

"Yes," she blushed and sniffed back her tears. "Yes, my dearest."

With that, Jamal placed the ring upon her finger and, as their eyes fluctuated from the stone and onto one another, their heads moved closer together. Then, Jamal placed his lips into the smooth, waiting crevice of her puckered mouth, and they kissed…with absolute, natural, love.

Mon·ster (mänstər)

noun: **monster**; plural noun: **monsters**

    1. an imaginary creature that is typically large, ugly, and frightening.

(So they say... So we keep hearing)

There's No Such Thing As Monsters
(Hearing)

September 11, 1993…

"…Gasoline prices are back down to normal since the effects of the Desert Storm conflict, from two years ago, have subsided. Experts predict a significant price drop per barrel over the next few years…"

On a street similar to yours, she is driving, just like you, excited like you, sometimes tired like you, but never too busy for the news. The static whirls and hisses as she changes from one news station to the next on her out of date radio. In between the static, her ears catch the lyrics to *Dirty Laundry* by Don Henley.

"…There's an eighty percent chance of rain tonight with a sixty percent chance of high temperatures later throughout the early morning, with a fifty percent chance of unknown weather by eight o'clock tomorrow morning…And by then, I might be able to look up in the sky, so you don't have to, and tell you what the weather will be on your drive to work!" sings the animated weather man, his smile almost visible through the radio, since she sees him every night on the television also.

Just now, she is passing a wonderful split level home, with the high steps you walk up to the front door, then open the door, go through, then go down the steps to an imaginary downstairs that is really on the same plane as the driveway that you walked up from. And on her left she is passing a wonderful split level home, with the high steps you walk up to the front door, then open the door, go through, then go down the steps to an imaginary downstairs that is really on the same plane as the driveway that you walked up from. And she is rolling quickly, at the recommended subdivision driving speed, past rows, on each side of her, of beautiful split level homes, with the high steps you walk up to the front door, then open the door, go through, then go down the steps to an imaginary downstairs that is really on the same plane as the driveway that you walked up from….but these are different colors. She is turning the corner on her street to see the Hot boys now walking outside, because the rain just stopped, as they are tucking in their iced necklaces, to wipe down their rides. And when they are pretty and shiny and wonderful and unique, when morning comes again they will have to wipe down their rides and rims from the night's sin, while the fast girls up town are on their knees, praying, wiping down their souls.

"Ahhh," she sighs, as she pulls up in front of her wonderful split level home, with the high steps you walk up to the front door, then open the door, go through, then go down the steps to an imaginary downstairs that is really on the same plane as the driveway that you walked up from. She smiles at her dream home that she and her husband built. When she first saw the design, out of the three designs that the three hundred home community offered, when she first looked at the plans that some architect, in his mind, had envisioned as a child and twisted and molded geometry in his head, she knew that it was her dream home. When she picked out the color of the choices she was given, and when they bought the only sized appliances that would fit in the spaces that the architect designed, and when she and her husband hung their pictures on the walls of the house where there were no windows (because who needs windows on every side of a house), she knew it was her dream home.

"…New information in the double murder suicide that we reported on yesterday," chants the newsman through the radio, "but first we will tell you thirty minutes of news from places and countries that don't concern you..."

"Oooo," she gulps, "I better get in the house! I don't want to miss this."

In the window beside the front door, the curtain is pulled back. An anxious faced little girl, Annie Child, stands pressed against the glass. Her eyes are as those of someone you know.

"Hello, my little baby!" the woman smiles, as she bends down to receive her two year old, crashing into her outstretched arms. "How are you? Did you enjoy staying home with Daddy today?"

"No-o-o!" the little two year old squeaks.

"Oh, did Daddy get on your nerves?" she laughs. "He was all sick and no fun, huh?" The little girl slightly nods yes and is clutching tightly around her mother's neck.

"Hey honey," the woman speaks to the man, who is reading the newspaper, as she walks into the den carrying the little girl in one arm and grocery bags in the other. "How was your day? Do you feel better?"

"Hey," he coughs. "Yeah, I guess it was a twenty-four hour bug. I'll probably go to work in the morning."

"Well, you hear that baby?" the woman says, swinging the little girl in the air. "You get to go to the nursery tomorrow. I bet you'd rather stay at home and spend another day with Daddy, huh?"

"No-o-o-o," the child begins to cry.

"Oh it's okay," the mother comforts. "Honey, did you spank her or something? She is awfully clingy and seems to be very upset with you."

"N-no. I didn't spank her. I, I just maybe chastised her... once."

"Oh I swear, every time she stays with you on your off days or sick days she is just so irritable. Well, I'm going to get dinner ready. Will you turn the news up so I can hear it in the kitchen?"

"Oh yeah, I fixed the little TV in the kitchen. Now we won't miss any of the news cast when we are in there."

"Great! Thank you honey! Dinner should be ready soon." The woman runs into the kitchen, still carrying her bags and her little girl.

Focusing his attention back towards the paper, the man's eyes read with rapid enthusiasm the story under the headline, *Technology Keeps Modern Kids Safe*. … 'With all the surveillance cameras, tracking devices built into back packs, computers, and phones, and with all the GPS enabled personal devices available, it's nearly impossible for today's child to be abducted or harmed by an outsider…'

Click, Zuomp! The kitchen television pops on.

"…Sitting in for Mitch Bolshot, I'm Liah Tella with your news, on this eleventh day of September, 1995. In world news tonight, a bomb exploded today in a shopping square where Serbians and Croatians were holding a peace rally. The detonation killed at least nine people, leaving seven others critically wounded. On hearing this report, a group of congressmen, representing the costal American states, began lobbying for better Homeland security here in the United States. Government security experts quickly shot down the idea, stating that with the technology available today, terrorist attacks within the continental U.S. are highly unlikely…"

"That's so awful," the woman says. "People killing each other because of their race or religion. Honey, did you hear that on the news?"

"Yeah! That's terrible," the man yells back from the living room. "That's why they're there and not here in America."

Back in the kitchen, the woman now has the food cooking.

"Honey, I'm going to get the mail," she yells to the man. "Now you have to let go of mommy while I go get the mail. Okay?" she tells the little girl.

"No-o-o," the little girl begins to cry again.

"I won't be long," the woman assures. "Go let Daddy hold you for…" The child screams and burst into flooding tears. "Okay, Annie, okay, come on," the woman gives in. She takes the little girl's hand and pulls the child close as the little girl quickly wraps hold of the woman's leg. With the child clinging to her leg, the woman walks awkwardly over to the cabinet above the microwave. From there, she pulls out two dust masks, two eye goggles, and one pair of latex gloves. She puts the goggles and mask on herself and on the little girl. Then the woman puts the latex gloves only on herself. She then picks up the little girl and carries her outside to the mailbox.

"Hi Mrs. Assumptions," the woman mutters through the dusk mask.

"Hello, how are you?" Mrs. Assumptions mumbles back through her own dusk mask. Mrs. Assumptions is walking out to get her mail also. She lives next door, alone. She does not have any children, but she greatly loves the little two year old girl. Mrs. Assumptions smiles beneath her mask and waves at the little girl. Mrs. Assumptions is so glad that the little girl is healthy and happy and growing up in a safe and loving environment. Mrs. Assumptions sees the woman and the man as very good and wonderful people. She would do anything to help them or the little girl. But as Mrs. Assumptions sees it, that family needs nothing.

The woman walks back into the house now. She has trained the little girl to close her eyes and cover her mouth whenever the mail is brought into the house. The little girl likes that game and is smiling now. The woman wipes off the mail with a damp cloth, opens all of it, and puts it in the microwave for a few minutes.

"Whew!" the woman sighs as she pulls off the mask and goggles.

"Woo!" the little girl mocks as she pulls off her goggles and mask, uncovering her smile.

"….Security experts for the United States," the newscaster boasts, "say that Sadam Hussein's threats of chemical warfare could never manifest within the continental U.S. so Americans should feel safe about handling foreign objects such as delivered packages and mail, now and in the future…"

"Honey? Did you hear that?" the woman yells to the living room.

"Yep. We can finally throw away those masks and gloves."

The mother now smiles and swings the little girl who also begins to laugh vigorously.

"Yay! Mommy doesn't have to use the masks anymore!" she chimes to the little girl. The mother tosses the masks, goggles, and gloves into the trash. Then she pulls her husband's goggles and mask from the cabinet and throws those away also.

The little girl is happy now. She's found a picture book to look at on the kitchen floor while her mother finishes making dinner. She makes sure that she is not too far away from the woman. As her little hands turn the pages, her little mind wonders what the letters and words are saying. She comes across a picture of a hairy monster.

"Look! See, Daddy, monster," she raises the picture to her mother.

"Daddy's a monster?" the woman smiles. "Yeah baby, he can be irritable when he's not feeling well." The woman turns back to her dinner preparation.

"No, no, look!" the little girl demands. "Daddy, monster."

"No sweetie, Daddy's not a monster. He just has a bad mood sometimes. There's no such thing as monsters. Now let Mommy finish, okay?"

Outside, like a row of dominos, the houses are all lined up; Split level homes, with the high steps you walk up to the front door, then open the door, go through, then go down the steps to an imaginary downstairs that is really on the same plane as the driveway that you walked up from. In the rear of the subdivision, Phase two is underway. More clone homes with a room change here or there to make them custom. The building permit and inspector sheet hangs at the front of each home under construction, with a notation: *Total Building Cost: $60,000.* In the model home across the street, the sales agent is handing a design layout to a prospective buyer, "These start at $170,000." That is okay, the Consumer Aid reporter on the news said that this is a great deal.

"Dinner's ready, honey," the woman calls out. The man springs up from the sofa and tunes his ears to the newscaster as he dashes from the living room to the dining room, not missing a word as he resumes his visual attention to the television on the wall in front of the dining table.

"...This just in: Gas prices will go up this week as much as thirty-five cents in most areas...."

"Hun?" the man, now puzzled, calls to his wife. "Did you check on the order for our storage containers?"

"The gas containers for Y2K?"

"Yes, those."

"They should be delivered this month."

The man breathes a sigh of relief as he smiles at the plate of food being set before him. Looking over at his little girl, sitting to his left, he smiles consolingly. She quickly frowns and looks down at her fingers fidgeting in her lap. The little girl is six years old now, with heavy thoughts on her mind. As the mother places her plate on the table and sits down, this is the time that a prayer is or is not said in your household too.

"...Last month," the female news anchor begins, "we told you how doctors have found that two cups of coffee in the morning can greatly increase a person's chance for heart failure and heart attack. Well, today more research shows that coffee at any time during the day may also put you at risk of these heart conditions..."

Before the newswoman can finish, the woman grabs her cup of coffee and jumps up from the table as the man hands her his cup. She pours them both into the sink, then reaches for the coffee containers in the cabinet and throws them in the trash on top of the mask and goggles. Tying up the trash bag, the woman looks back at the dining table, "Annie, baby? I know you don't feel good but you have to eat some food." The little girl takes a spoonful of food and slowly chews. She continues to look down at her fingers still fidgeting in her lap.

"I think she is coming down with the bug you had," the woman suggest as she sits back down at the table with two glasses of water.

"I, I don't think so," the man says, staring at his daughter.

"Then what do you think is wrong?" the woman searches.

The man looks back at the woman and offers, "Yeah, maybe you're right, maybe she is catching a hint of my bug."

The six o'clock news cast concludes with local sports and the weather for the week. "...I'm Liah Tella, and thank you for watching WBS4U evening news..."

This is the time when prime time television shows begin.

"That's enough entertainment for a couple of hours," the woman says as she turns off the television. She and the man are enjoying the meal in relative quiet. Every now and then they discuss the woman's day at work or the man's day at home. Every now and then they smile or laugh, as you do at your dinner table.

"Annie? Annie Child? Straighten up and sit up right. You'll ruin your posture," the woman scolds. "You won't look nice when you get older and we put you on one of those *marry a millionaire* shows. A potential husband won't like that."

"Oh yes, Annie, yes," the man agrees. "Please, sit up straight."

After dinner, they are cleaning up and preparing for the next day and for the evening news.

"Annie, baby, do you want to help Daddy wash the dishes?" the woman asks.

"No," the little seven year old whispers.

"Okay, then it's time for me to help you with your bath. You have to go to school tomorrow."

In the tub, the woman helps the little girl bathe. Then the woman brushes the girl's hair and tells her how beautiful she is and enjoys mother and daughter time together. This is the happiest time of the day for the little girl. She is smiling endlessly.

"Hey you," the man says, poking his head in through the door with a playful grin. "You getting your bath? Is Mommy giving you a bath?"

The little girl averts her eyes and nods. Her endless smile disappears. She leans toward her mother on the outside of the tub.

"Guess she's still mad at you," the woman jokes. "That's right baby, don't pay Daddy any attention. This is mother and daughter time."

Outside it has begun to rain again. In the near distance, lightning flashes and faint cracks of thunder can be heard. The Hot boys and the want-to-be followers, have covered their rides and sit inside their homes blasting *Dirty Laundry*, by Don Henley on their house stereos.

Out of the tub and all cozy in bed, the little girl lies on her pillow as the woman reads her a story. It is the story of a princess, the story of little pigs, the story of how the stork brought her, and the story of a brave warrior. The little girl smiles and laughs and hopes. And now, it is time to dream.

"Okay baby, time to go to sleep," the woman says at the end of the story.

"No-o-o-o," the little girl begins to cry, "No-o-o, mommy please!"

"Come on now, not tonight," the woman pleads.

"No mommy, the monster!"

The woman lets out a sigh. She is exhausted from a long day of working away and at home. "Do you want the night light on?" the woman asks, but the little girl shakes her head. "Do you want the hall light on, or your flashlight?" Again, the little girl shakes her head, now crying silently. "Okay then. You have to go to sleep. You've got school tomorrow," the woman orders.

"No, mommy, please!"

"Annie Child! You listen to your mother!" the woman demands. Then, she catches herself, takes a deep breath and speaks softly, "There is no such thing as monsters."

The little girl stops crying out loud and buries her face in the pillow. Her heart is beating fast. She is terrified and feels so alone. *Why can't Mommy see?* Outside, it is raining harder now and the lightning and thunder has moved closer.

Down stairs in the living room, the man and woman begin watching the eleven o'clock news.

"…And that's your Local weather for tomorrow. I'll be back later with the National. Tom, back to you."

"Thanks Dick. We'd like to update you on an earlier story. We reported this afternoon that coffee, in any amount during anytime can lead to serious heart conditions. Within a few hours of that broadcast, our sponsor, ahem, I mean, scientist have discovered that coffee does not, I repeat, does not contribute to heart failure and heart attack after all…."

"Hun?" the man calls to the woman.

"I'm getting the coffee containers out of the trash," she replies.

"I was just about to do that. I'll buy a lot more tomorrow. I'll fill up one of the shelves in the pantry with just coffee."

The woman soon returns with two searing hot cups and sits down beside the man on the sofa.

"…In social issues today," the makeup matted, bleached blonde anchorwoman begins, "recent polls show that lately there have been no reports of any child abuse cases involving members of the same family. So it is something parents do not have to worry about…"

The woman smiles and takes the man's hand to hold in hers. She feels so secure with him because of the news.

"…No reported cross burnings lately. Many American citizens feel that the Ku Klux Klan, was, in the past, wrongly accused of events such as cross burnings on non-Klan property. Many also feel that the Klan is an organization which has helped the progress of many groups of minorities and of all nationalities. Last month, two historically black colleges, in the South East, received anonymous multi-million donations toward their scholarship funds…"

"… AIDS, and HIV, the disease that causes AIDS, has not been a major topic the way it was when the epidemic was first made known to mainstream media. The word from the medical field is that the percentage of people infected with AIDS has risen, but as usual, we here at WBS4U ask the question, 'Are doctors always right?' There have been no multitude cases of AIDS related deaths lately, almost as if it didn't exist. 'Maybe today's medical reports are in error,' say society's experts…"

"…Some good news for Americans here and abroad: While in Cairo, on February 24, Colin Powell, US Secretary of State, stated 'Saddam Hussein has not developed any significant capability with respect to weapons of mass destruction. He is unable to project conventional power against his neighbors.' Again on May 15, Powell stated that it was the US policy of 'containment' that had effectively disarmed Hussein and that Saddam Hussein had not been able to 'build his military back up or to develop weapons of mass destruction' for 'the last 10 years'. America, has been successful in keeping him 'in a box'. Now, in this month of July, 2001, Condoleezza Rice has described a weak, divided and militarily defenseless Iraq. 'Saddam does not control the northern part of the country,' she said. 'We are able to keep his arms from him. His military forces have not been rebuilt since Dessert Storm.' …"

"Well that's great," the man says. "Of all the terrorist in the world, if they ever attacked us, we know we wouldn't have to waste time going to Iraq…"

"Mommy, Daddy," Annie startles them from behind the sofa, "can we watch that new late night reality show?"

"Sweetie," the woman answers, "I thought you went to bed? I know that you're sixteen now, but you still need to get your sleep for school…"

"And for your beauty rest; to look presentable in case you get discovered by a talent agent that may happen to walk by," joins the man.   The young girl narrows her eyes and gives the man a deadly stare.

"Besides," the woman continues, "This is Universal News. It tells us everything that is happening all over!"

"Yeah, we can't miss this!" adds the man.

Sixteen year old Annie sighs and looks away. Then she rebounds, "I don't know why you both watch that crap day in and day out. You don't even listen to your own discernment. You just let the media think for you. I mean, media molds public opinion!"

The woman and the man look at each other puzzled for a moment. Then both break into hysterical laughter.

"Oh Annie, baby, you are such a comedian!" laughs the woman.

"*Media molds public opinion!*" mocks the man, "C'mon! Get out of here!"

"It's true," Annie continues. "The news and informative media tell you what they want you to know in a way to make you believe, act, say, or buy, what they want you to. They're puppet masters and you, me, and everyone else are the puppets! You are a puppet, Mommy!"

"That's it!" yells the man. "You've gone too far! I suppose next you'll, you'll be saying that there are monsters in this house!"

Annie folds her arms, cocks her head, and raises an eyebrow at the man.

"The news said that teenagers are so rebellious!" the woman says nodding towards the man.

"O-M-G, mommy! Deal with me and *my* mind, not the stereotypical media profile!"

"Go to your room!" the man orders.

The woman and the man enjoy the rest of the news cast. They get a recap of the weather, local and national. They see the triumphs and joys of others around the world. They are also captivated by other's failures and pain. They are shocked and horrified by the sufferings of others, but they cannot look away. In the end, they are very pleased and satisfied when the anchor woman says, "Well, that's what American society says, and that's the way it is. Good night."

With the end of the nightly news cast, the woman and the man turn off all the lights, lock all the doors, and accompany one another to their bedroom. As they prepare for sleep, with showers, brushing of teeth, and other learned rituals, the woman turns on the big screen television, hanging on the wall in front of her bed. As she flips through the seemingly endless choice of channels, the man strokes her hair with an occasional kiss to her forehead. As she flips through the channels, she pauses often, turns and smiles at the man, whom she loves with all her heart. All light in the house is absent, except for the flickering glow from the television.

As her eyes are slowly becoming heavier, the woman slumps down lower from the headboard to resting on the pillow. Taking the man's hand in hers, she is kissing it tenderly. In her other hand, the preset channel surfing is slowing its pace: sports news, food news, medical news, home news...

The flash of lightning through her curtain-less window illuminates the room of Annie Child. She doesn't jump anymore because of the thunder and the lightning. In her sixteen years she has learned that there are far more scary things of the dark and when alone. She is on her knees, with hands clasped tightly beneath her head, bending down over her bed. With her eyes closed but with ears wide open to the entrance of her room, where the monster will soon appear, she shivers and she prays. You would think that the woman would see the monster after all these years, but the news reports don't believe in them so why should she?

The woman awakes to the sound of a late night movie which trailed the late night news. Half asleep, she fondles behind her near the middle of the bed, searching for the remote. Clicking off the television she vaguely realizes that the man is not in bed. *He usually checks on Annie in the middle of the night*, she remembers. Then, from down the hall, comes a faint whimper, which the woman dismisses as Annie laughing in her dreams, because the woman knows that there is no such thing as monsters. The woman smiles and fades back into sleep.

Next door, Mrs. Assumptions lies down to sleep. She smiles at the good things in her life, like knowing she has good neighbors like the man and woman and the young girl. She smiles as she thinks of them as the perfect family, although, she wishes the young girl would put her curtains back up so that her bedroom light would not keep Mrs. Assumptions awake some nights. Mrs. Assumptions can see clear into Annie Child's bedroom at night. She often wonders why the girl took down her curtains. "The news did say kids are rude and rebellious at that age," she reasons. "Hmph! Teenagers!" Mrs. Assumptions does not have children and does not believe in monsters. But even if she had children, Mrs. Assumptions watches the news every morning and every night so she probably wouldn't believe in monsters until one took her child away, somewhere, in her town, in a town like yours, where discernment has been replaced.

Every fresh start begins with, "Take a deep breath."

Rain Dogs
(Smell)

As I opened my eyes to the tan and light chocolate coordinate colored room, now filled with the morning light, I knew something was wrong. Ever since we've been married, I have always awakened the same way, as if subconsciously programed to reach across to my husband, lying beside me, while opening my eyes. Maybe it comes from the unbreakable union of love that we've built; our every thought revolves around the other's happiness. And when I would awake, he would always be lying there, staring at me with those large wonderful brown eyes and wearing a smile which could barely be noticed, just a slight curve on the edges. It was as if he was so amazed at me. I would always smile as I looked at the first sight of my day –the beautiful face of Bobby Calhoun.

I once asked him why was it that he always awoke before me and why did he lay there and stare at me. He told me that he often wondered if he was worthy to have someone like me, and he drenched my heart with compliments. Next he told me that he wanted 'to make sure the world was safe enough and happy enough before I entered it for the day, because if it wasn't he would hold me and sing me right back to sleep until everything was alright for his queen.' He is so silly yet full of romance. Maybe it's because we've only been married for four and a half years that the candle still burns bright. Or maybe our relationship is truly strong and irrepressible. I love that man!

Yeah, four and a half years of being Mrs. Cassie Calhoun, and each morning had been more wonderful than the one before. On this morning, however, as I reached over and opened my eyes, there was nothing but the morning light and empty space. I knew something was too wrong.

Now, Bobby still hadn't broken his habit of being there beside me every morning. Between me and his side of the bed lay our daughter, Mouse, who was a perfect representation of his heart. Bobby nicknamed her Mouse because she was short like me and she was small and wouldn't stop wiggling around since the day she was born; always moving and scurrying, getting into the tiniest holes or spaces that she could find, always trying to hide. Her real name is Amanda, which means 'to be loved.' Her middle name is Brook. Yeah, that's right, 'To be loved by the brook.' Maybe it's corny or comical but that's my hopeless romantic husband. *I love that man!* She was his 'daddy's little girl' who he was proudly turning into 'daddy's little tom-boy.' Barely three years old and he already had her wearing baseball caps turned to the back and tank tops which were clearly designed for little boys. Even the toys he bought were obviously for boys like the rocket ships and dump trucks she used to blow up and run over the dolls that I bought for her. Bobby was even building her, brace yourself, a go-cart! He promised me that he wouldn't let her ride by herself until she was ten. I wanted the age of fourteen or fifteen but as we always do we compromised, which still kept me satisfied since it wasn't going to be the age of six – his initial request.

At first, I was surprised that she was still asleep. Then I remembered the thunder storm which had kept her awake and crying all night. She looked so innocent and cute, coiled up with her curly black hair and warm light skinned complexion which were both just like mine. She looked more like me all over except for her eyes. Now, I have green eyes but hers are like her father's, brown… large, soft, inviting brown.

Mouse awoke as I slowly stroked her curly hair. She looked at me, then slowly towards Bobby's side of the bed, and back at me with a look of bewilderment.

"I know sweetheart, I know," I whispered. I reasoned that in the times that she had slept in our bed she had always awakened with him by her side also. Still groggy and speechless from sleep, she only stared at his pillow.

****

The sky was clear and the sun light rolled up the back of my black car as I opened the garage door.

"I want daddy, momma, I want daddy," Mouse was whining from her car seat.

"Alright, alright, we're going to go get him."

The streets were still wet with clouds of mist rising above them. On both sides of the road lay the April batch of bright green grass and pretty color filled flowers, cloaked with rain drops. It was such a beautiful day, too beautiful, too perfect.

As we drove, Mouse sang and talked the entire time. Every now and then she would turn to me and yell, 'I want daddy, momma!' Of the three of us, she was the most talkative. Sure, Bobby was limitlessly romantic in emotion and action but brief in words. He was shy – more so reserved, but with his smiles, his hugs and the dancing of his large brown eyes he could express himself better than anyone. Yet, I was just about the only one who could understand him. To those who didn't know him he would appear to be kind of a loner, except when it came to Mouse and me. I know without a doubt that we were his most loved and no one could ever convince me of otherwise.

Approaching the Panola Hills parking lot, a quick glance told me that he wasn't there. *Still, his truck might be around back,* I hoped. I eased around the narrow drive to the back lot and suddenly, from the corner of the building, appeared a large, soggy, dirty looking dog. I braked quickly and it stopped and stared at the car then slowly walked on, head down, and tail between its legs. Its ribs were visible at its midsection.

"Wain dog, momma, Wain dog," Mouse reminded me as it caught her attention. A couple of days earlier, Bobby had told her about a stray dog which had wandered through our neighborhood one drizzling morning. "Look momma, look!" He had explained to her how when a dog strays from home he marks areas along the way so that he can sniff his way back. Sometimes it rains and washes away the scent, and if the dog is far away or in a place that he's never been before, he can't find his way home. He just wanders from doorstep to doorstep looking for his home. Now that's a lot for a three year old but that was Bobby's way. *Talk to children like regular people, not with baby talk and they will learn quicker* or something like that. I think the only part she remembered was that a wet dog is a rain dog and that a rain dog is a wet dog.

After cruising through the back lot, still with no sign of Bobby, we headed to the only other place he could be, the place I had wished he was not, the one place I knew he had to be. I just wished he wasn't there. *Why couldn't he have been here, at Panola Hills?* Panola Hills is where I work as an administrator. It's a home for severely and terminally ill children. Bobby volunteers there part-time. That's where we met. I remember the first day he started working there. To be honest, I had serious concerns when I saw this grown, funny looking man wanting to spend time with sick children. And since he was doing this for free I wondered about his motives. Now, of course, I don't think my husband is funny looking! Back then I was just little Miss Perfect, with perfect plans for a perfect life, and Bobby Calhoun did not appear to me as the perfect man. Bobby, however, quickly changed my outlook on life. I remember every moment of that day…

"Mrs. Liz? Mrs. Liz!" I called.

"Yes Cassie, what is it child?" My elder coworker appeared in the doorway of my office with three stuffed animals cradled in her arms.

"Mrs. Liz, it's ten till one. Isn't it story time? Why are those children making so much noise? I can't get any work done! I keep…"

"Child, you stress yourself daily! Oh lord, will she ever relax? The children ARE having story time as usual."

"Well, they've never been so noisy during a book reading."

"Child, that's not noise! That's laughter, the sound of healing. And you know these children need all the healing they can get. Come now, see for yourself"

Mrs. Liz practically dragged me from my desk and down the hall to the large playroom where every day most of the children listened to a story. As I made my way through the crowd of nurses crammed in the doorway my heart sunk and began to race.

"Carlos!" I screamed. "Get down baby, please!" The sickest child in the whole facility was out of his wheel chair and climbing with the other kids on the back of a strange man. I quickly picked him up and sat him down in his chair to check his pulse. He seemed so weak and his heart was beating so fast. "Mrs. Liz, how could you let him exert himself like this? Why are all of you standing around?" I shouted at the other nurses. "Help me get these children calmed down!"

"But they are so happy. They've never had so much fun," Lashawn said.

"Look Mrs. Thang, we are responsible for their health not their fun. And don't question my authority ever again. Are we clear?"

"Yes Ma'am," she said and walked away. Okay, so I was kind of overbearing back then, but I had to be. We were dealing with little lives. Looking back now, it seemed as if I had sucked the sunshine out of the room. Everyone was either dejected or angry. Everyone, except for the strange man who had been the center of the commotion. There he was, still bent down on the floor, with his head cocked slightly to the side and with those large eyes dancing at me from behind his glasses. And to really pis me off he had a huge grin on his face.

"And who might you be?" I asked.

"Bobby, Bobby Calhoun. I'm the new volunteer."

"Oh yeah, you're the one Mrs. Liz approved while I was on vacation last week. Hmmmm, from now on maybe I should oversee the approval of *all* the volunteers and employees."

"Is there a problem with me?" He replied, still wearing his goofy grin.

"Well, for one thing you don't let sickly children overexert themselves!"

"The children are fine," he quickly said. He actually talked back to me! I couldn't believe that two people had talked back to me in one day. For some reason though, with him I couldn't address it. I didn't really know why.

"Well, Mr. Calhoun, take a look at Carlos here. He is sweating and his heart was racing when I first picked him up…"

"He is very weak, I know. That's why I kept him close to me and made sure Mrs. Liz and the others were here to watch him. He's okay. He's just excited. Look at his smile."

"First of all don't cut me off again. Second, I'm sure he is exhausted from your little animated interactive story! Michelle, take Carlos back to his room and get…"

Carlos leapt from his chair and ran over and hugged Bobby tightly, "Thank you for the story Mr. Bobby!" Then he ran back and jumped into his wheel chair, "Okay Mrs. Michelle, I ready now. Push me!"

"Touché," someone in the room whispered, joined by a light chuckle.

"Okay," I demanded, "Everyone get these children to where they need to be and go back to work. Mr. Calhoun, I need to see you in my office."

As we walked into my office I had it all planned out how to rip him and make him understand who I was and what his responsibility was: doing as I instructed him to and that only. But we sat down and I sort of lost some of the things I wanted to say. Maybe it was the smile that seemed to be permanently glued to his face, or maybe, unknown to me at the time I was so lost in his large brown eyes that I just could not be hard with him.

"Ma'am," he started, "I know you are concerned about me and my qualifications. Since you really have lots of work to do now, how about I take you for a bite to eat after work and I can answer all of your questions. There is a great new café on Jonesboro Road called Big Momma's. We could sit down without having to worry about time and you could tell me what I need to know, like exactly what my responsibilities are and let me know if I should do those and *only* those. *You* are the head person. I need to know what *you* require me to do."

Okay, he was good. I convinced myself that I was not going out on a date or anything, it was strictly a business meeting. After all, I did have a lot of work to catch up on, and I did need to know more about this stranger who would be around the children. Besides, aside from his nice eyes and smile he definitely was not my type physically. He's kind of, well, it's not important. So I agreed, reluctantly. But I didn't smile when I said okay. I had to show who was in charge.

When I walked into Big Momma's, I immediately had this homey cozy feeling and the food smelled wonderful.

"Hello," said the hostess. "How many in your party?"

"I'm supposed to meet someone here. He may already be here but I don't see him."

"What's the name?"

"Calhoun, Bobby Calhoun."

Immediately, the hostess seemed to smile the big goofy grin I had noticed earlier on Bobby.

"Yes ma'am, he is already here. Right this way."

She led me to a table already set for two and handed me a menu. *This is nice*, I thought. *But don't forget what you came here for. This is business.*

"Well, hello," Bobby said as he appeared from out of nowhere and pressed himself in between the stationary seat and table.

"Would you like to sit at another table with more room?" I teased.

"No," he smiled back. "This is fine. I sit here often. It helps me work harder at losing some of this gut."

Some? I thought to myself. "So have you ordered yet?"

"No. I was waiting on you."

"Oh, what a gentleman," I mumbled with much sarcasm.

We ordered our food. Bobby had the Big Momma's hot wing special, while I opted for something simple –a chicken wrap. When the food came I noticed that his plate had a little extra, well, a lot of extra wings, more than what the menu stated.

"Uh, they must like you," I snooped. "Do you eat here a lot?"

"Yeah. Oh yeah," he said brandishing that goofy grin of his.

"So Mr. Calhoun, why are you interested in working at a home filled with sick children? Why not volunteer at the Boy Scouts or the Y?"

"All about business, huh? Let's get right to it then," he smiled. "I love children. I don't have any of my own but I hope to someday. I want to work with sick children because I think they need someone more than the kids in the Scouts or at the Y. Besides, I know what it's like when you really need someone to care and no one does."

When he said that, my heart seemed to feel whatever his past was holding. Maybe it was the way his grin disappeared so fast or how his eyes looked dazed.

"Were you a sick child, Mr. Calhoun?"

"Yes. Asthma. I started having daily breathing treatments when I was six years old… just in time for first grade. Huh, school, kids can be so cruel." His eyes were now looking down at the table. As he slowed his chews it was as if his past had come up and smacked him from behind. There was something heavy on his mind.

"Mr. Calhoun, are you okay?" I offered.

"Yes. I did have one person always there that made a world of difference." He began smiling again. I could tell that he wasn't just talking about someone being there through *asthma*.

"So, back to the children. There are so many responsibilities and so many undesirable duties that come from working there at the home. It is not all play and laughter. And many times we deal with, well, death. Losing one of those children can sometimes take a lot out of anyone. Do you know exactly what you are getting into, Mr. Calhoun?"

There was a brief silence as he stared towards the corner of the table. Then, as his large brown eyes rose up to rest in mine and his smile seemed to reach out and caress the side of my face he, said, "Just because a rose has thorns, you wouldn't cut it down would you?"

And that was the beginning of the end of my shallow views of Mr. Bobby Calhoun. With his boyish charm and humbleness he would soon erase all of my immature thoughts toward him, like a steamroller paving the way into my heart...

****

I arrived at the one last place I knew he would be. At 1746 Ivy Street, a home and many memories were about to be demolished. This was the house where Bobby grew up. His grandmomma had raised him since the age of four. That's when he had lost his parents in a car accident. Everyone had said that it was by divine intervention Bobby's father had, at the last moment, wanted him to stay behind with his grandmomma. After all, his parents were heading to a discount toy outlet to buy one of those large plastic play castles for Bobby. Bobby says he has a clear memory of that day from his childhood, seeing his mother slowly get into the car looking sad and anxious as if she knew she would never see her little boy again. His father had been too stern to turn and look at him, not really being able to explain why. He didn't explain his reason to anyone. But everyone had just accepted it. Even Bobby's mother didn't question him. She had only climbed into the dirty old Chevy, leaving her heart there behind, his little hands holding tightly to the wooden post of the front porch, with eyes full of tears.

After the accident his grandmomma raised him. From what I've seen and heard they became closer than any natural mother and son could be. I guess, in a way that is *natural* when your parents, your providers of security and direction, are suddenly torn away from you before you are even old enough to understand the imprint upon them which you are old enough to have. Bobby was always a quick adapter though. That made him strong for lots of things. But sometimes, even the pillars of stone get cracks and have to be reinforced.

Yeah, it was always Bobby and his grandmomma, according to everyone who knew him before me. He was always her little helper; always there ready to do a task for her, especially when she would promise him a 'box of five-irons.'

'Bobbeeeeeeeeeee!' she would yell in an opera like tone, and he would come dashing to her side. Although most neighbors said she rarely had to call for him, because he stayed on her coat tails all the time.

'Yes?' he would gleam. I can just imagine that cute dark brown, round child's face but still having those large brown eyes.

'I got a box of five-irons. You want some five-irons?' she would ask.

'Yes!' his face would be all lit up with his eyes filled with anticipation.

'Well, I need you to help your Big Momma out. Some stray dogs got into the trash cans last night and spread trash all around the back door. Take this bag and get it all up for me, baby. Okay? And then I'll give you a box full of five-irons!' Everyone said he would smile and laugh the whole time that he was doing whatever task she had asked him to do. He was Big Momma's little soldier then, and she was his Big Momma. He loved her so much he had named his restaurant after her. That's right, Big Momma's was his. He told me about his ownership after about two weeks of us getting to know each other. But, that first day when I had met him there, I think I already knew.

Everyone that works there always has an unbreakable smile and the atmosphere is so comforting. You just want to stay there and leave your troubles outside. That is how I've always felt around Bobby. I don't think anyone can care as much for other people as he does.

When his task was done Bobby would race to his grandmomma's side to let her know that he was finished so he could get his box of five-irons.

'Okay,' Big Momma would say. 'Lay down on the floor.' He would lay down, giggling and twitching the whole time. Then she would bend down, reach out with her open palm and count out each finger as she folded them down into a fist and twisted it into his stomach to tickle him and make him laugh so hard tears would come to his eyes, 'One, two, three, four, five!' It meant the world to him. You can trick a child into doing something and give them a box of five-irons one time. It used to baffle the nosey neighbors why he would always do anything for a box of five-irons. He wasn't being fooled. It just meant the world to him to laugh with Big Momma. *She* meant the world to him.

At 1746 Ivy Street, Peach State Power had bought, or should I say forced Bobby to sell, his grandmomma's land and house so that they could build another transmission tower to carry power from one of their nearby substations. They had bought most of the homes around his grandmomma's house, and Bobby had been the last to sell. It was so hard for him to let go of a place he had always thought would be there.

As I got closer to the house I noticed a bulldozer, backhoe, and dump truck, a couple of small utility vehicles, a fire truck, and two police cars pulling up in front of me.

"Daddy, momma! Daddy!" Mouse started. She had loosed herself from the rear child seat, as she always does, and was pressed against the glass staring at Bobby's truck parked in the gravel driveway.

"B-momma house," she said as I lifted her from the back seat. She had been here many times before and recognized where we were.

With Mouse in my arm I made my way toward the old house.

"Okay, what's the problem," one of the officers asked.

An older man, with a huge white beard, wearing a hard hat stepped forward in anger, "The problem is some fat S-O-B has barricaded himself in the rear of the house and said he's not gonna let us tear it down!"

"Sir, you need to calm down," butted in the other officer.

"I'm sorry. But I just have a job to do. So if you would please, arrest his fat ass so I can…"

"My husband is not fat!" I said looking directly into his hateful eyes. His eyes opened sharply but then quickly looked away from me while his hands began searching for pockets that were never there.

"Ma'am, is your husband the man inside the house?" the second officer asked.

"I'm pretty sure it's him," I smiled.

"Is he armed?" the first younger officer blurted, turning towards the old bearded man in the hard hat.

"He might be!" he answered, then he quickly glanced at the whip-ass expression on my face. "But I don't think he is." His hands began searching even harder for those pockets.

"Ma'am, what's your husband's name?" the second officer asked, pulling out a small note pad.

"His name is Bobby. Bobby Calhoun."

Have you ever noticed how when the flag is raised or when the national anthem is sung some people get all misty eyed or full of spirit? Have you ever seen a baby bird, kitten, or puppy and gotten that warm, fuzzy feeling inside? Well, when I said Bobby's name, I think it had that same effect on just about everyone there. The firemen, who had walked up to the conversation, started smiling. The driver of the dump truck standing nearby took off his shades and went from looking scruffy to childlike in his face with a warm smile. And the second older policeman smiled with excitement and quickly put away his note pad.

"Bobby? That's Bobby in there?" gleamed the older policeman. Bobby had helped the policeman with his son in a youth camp about a year ago. And when the county had halted public service funding because of the economy, Bobby had helped raise money for County policemen to upgrade their bullet proof vests by having a huge cookout. He had provided food for the Fireman's Association volunteers at a *Give Burns the Boot* walk-a-thon a few months ago. And yes, even the dump truck driver knew of Bobby. Some time ago he was on the verge of losing his small business and Bobby had given him a personal loan. Bobby meant a great deal to each one of them. Their anxious expressions all disappeared when they found out that it was Bobby. The situation was no longer some crazy man held up in a house about to be demolished, but now it was a friend who needed help.

I was allowed to go through to talk with Bobby. The old man with the white beard of course was incensed and threatened them all. Still, Mouse and I went right up to the house. I had been there many times before. It was always so peaceful, though, now it looked worn and ready to crumple and fade out of existence.

Looking at the boarded up house from the front I saw no easy entry way. I walked around to the back of the house. There was a large piece of plywood covering half of the window of what used to be Big Momma's room. It had been nailed up from the inside. There was enough space between the board and window to see the beautiful dark brown face of my husband. I could also see those beautiful tear tracks still fresh on his face as he sat there on the floor by the window.

"Hey you," I whispered. He looked up startled. *Didn't you know I would come for you?* I wanted to say. As I stared for a moment into his worn face and sleepless eyes, even with the burdens of the world he held along with his own, I could still see the hint of an answering smile. That's why I loved him so much.

"Daddy!" Mouse shouted. It took her a moment to really focus on the man sitting there behind a half-barricade. But nothing could keep her from recognizing her daddy, even without his glasses, which were in his lap.

Bobby sniffed and wiped his face, then gently slid his glasses on.

"Hey baby," he softly spoke. "How are both my girls?" There was anxiety and desperation in his voice. I wanted to just hold him. I wanted to cry, but he needed a shoulder right then. I had to hold it back.

"What's going on, Bobby?"

He looked down quickly. His hands were clasped together and fidgeting in his lap.

"I can't," he hesitated, "I can't let go. This is my home. What am I going to do when it's torn down? It's, it's all my fault."

"What's your fault, Bobby?"

"Selling the house. That's when, that's when she died." His tears had begun again. When Peach State power convinced him to sell the house, Big Momma moved in with us. She died soon after. A mentally and seemingly physically powerful lady seemed to just wilt away when she had moved out of that house. It had only been a few months since her death and he was still placing guilt on himself. "I'm tired of losing everything. I'm tired of losing everyone. This is all I have." He lost his grandmomma and months before that, Carlos, lost his battle with leukemia. He was nine years old. "This is the only place I could come when things got bad. Growing up, all the kids used to make fun of me because of my weight. I could always come home, here, and Big Momma always made me feel loved. I was always wanted here. It was always my home."

"Baby, *we* have a home, and now you have other family; you have Mouse and me and lots of other people who have come to love you…"

"I know, I know, but it's different. I just need a piece of her, of this house to still be here. This house was here for every body. Somebody always needed a place to stay or needed food or something and we were always here for them. Like Steve and Cindy. Who said that they could call *my* Big Momma, Momma anyway?" He seemed to try and be mad at them, reaching for another emotion other than sadness. "This house was here for everybody and now it's not going to be here for me." Bobby was all huddled up, the same way the nurses found him holding Carlos's body when he died at Panola Hills. Carlos was an orphan and Bobby became his only family. When his condition had started to worsen, Bobby had stayed by his side as often as he could, reading every book Carlos loved, over and over.

He was looking down away from me the whole time that he talked. He never did that before. No matter his reserved spirit, he always looked right into my eyes whenever he spoke to me. I knew he was really depressed. I wanted to tell him that it would be alright and that he had all those people who loved him and who were there for him. But he needed to realize it for himself. It hurt me so much to see him like that. I wanted to cry with him but he needed more, he needed something firm.

"Bobby," I said stiffly, "What's your philosophy of life?"

He looked up at me with eyes full of tears.

"Cassie, I'm not..."

"Just answer it. You asked me that when we were dating. I told you mine and you told me yours. I just want to hear it again."

He sighed and stared down at his lap again.

"The greatest joy," he stammered, "the greatest joy within the experience of life is giving, which completes the circle of purpose, being that life itself is a gift."

"Where did you learn that from? You never told me."

"It's too long of a story."

"Don't worry, you're *friends* out there will give you all the time you need."

He looked up at me startled again, searching my face for reason. Then he looked down, sighed and sniffed. "No one ever told me that. I just learned it from Big Momma... There was this one time especially, when she asked me to do something for her. I was all excited, thinking I was gonna get a box of five-irons. Instead she gave me this real pretty polished stone. See, this other time before that, when I was mad about everybody coming to live here, I asked why we always had to help them and she promised to tell me later. So the next time, when she gave me the stone, she said that it was strong and firm and it could support. She said that sometimes in life people needed other people to be their support or be their family or strong foundation for a moment. She liked helping others or being there for them. She asked if I liked doing tasks and favors for her. I said yes, because of the five-irons. She asked if I would still do it even without the five-irons. I said yes, because it made her happy. She asked if that truly made me happy. I said yes. She said that to her I was like that stone or rock, and one day I might have to be that rock to many others. And the more people I was there for the more happiness I would have." He raised his palms to bury his face and began to cry harder now though still silent for Mouse's sake. "I came here to see if I could find that stone, to have something to remember her by. But when I got here, I just got lost in all the memories, and I don't want to leave."

"Baby," I whispered, "you are that stone."

"No," he shook his head. "I can't be."

I could no longer hold back my tears. I was holding Mouse who was frowning at my face. *I'm his wife. This is MY husband,* I screamed in my head. Everything in me didn't want to but I knew I had to, so I slipped Mouse in through the small opening between the board and the window.

"Daddy, daddy!"

"Cassie, what are you doing?" he looked up quickly.

Mouse immediately squeezed her arms around her daddy's neck. Then, she began wiping the tears from his face and kissing his face all over just as he had done to her a million times before.

"Cassie, get her. I don't want her to see me like this!" he begged. I stayed silent and tried to smile through my tears. "Cassie, please, take her."

"Baby," I said, "you just got lost for a moment. Just look around you and your home is right there. You know which way to go. I believe in you." With every pain I've ever known seeming to flare up inside me, I closed my eyes and turned around. *He will come out cause he won't let Mouse be in harm's way,* I reasoned. *But what if he doesn't? I have to knock down that board. I have to get in there!* I was breathing so hard and my pulse was racing. I made up in my mind that I was going to turn around and lunge forward against that board and break it down. Unlike the others, it was nailed from the inside, so I knew it would give. I might break every fingernail, or cut up my hands and arms but that was *my* husband! In my head I saw me going through every motion. The whole time Bobby kept pleading with me.

"Cassie? Please get her out of here, please."

Ready to turn and lunge, ready to throw my entire body and spirit against that board, before I turned back towards Bobby, I opened my eyes and froze. My trance, my plan, my adrenaline were sucked away, as I was surprised to see another older Policeman standing in front of me. He was another white male, medium height, who looked to be in his early sixties. He just stared at me. He didn't look angry or agitated or rushed. He just stared at me. With his eyes he searched my tear soaked face, as if wondering how to arrest a woman, a man, and their child. And then, his face just changed. That same comforting grin that I had seen on the other older policeman slowly formed on his lips. I think he had been there the whole time, listening to our conversation. Behind him, more policeman, who had arrived, were walking toward us. My heart was pounding and I swallowed so hard my throat burned. Then, the older policeman raised his hand and pointed in the direction behind me and nodded, still smiling. I whipped myself around to see two sets of hands pulling back the board from the inside of the house with cracking and squeaking of wood and nails. Two firemen, escorted by other policemen had pried through the boards on the front of the house and entered the room where Bobby and Mouse sat huddled together. One of the policeman who had entered the room looked out at me, then at the older policeman behind me.

"Now what sir?"

I turned back towards the older policeman. Now I was searching him with my eyes. The small group of S.W.A.T members were now beside him, no weapons, no masks, no shields, just stern looks. *Yeah, now what,* I thought, ready to pounce and defend my husband and child.

"Now we help him," he said so softly.

"Captain?" the policeman inside questioned.

"We will all help Bobby find his stone." He smiled at me.

I wanted to faint. My adrenaline had gone from determination, to surprise, to fear, to anger, and now dead nothing. I wanted to drop to my knees and faint. "Mr. Calhoun here," he said turning to the policeman and the firefighters beside him and inside the room, "lost a tiny polished stone. We will all help Mr. Calhoun find that stone. It's in this house. Look in every crack and every corner."

I turned around and looked at my husband, whose face was flushed and confused. His eyes, still full of water, were large and wide again. And Mouse, still clinging tightly to him looked at me and said, "We help daddy." And then turned to him, "We help you now daddy."

There is an old saying, 'home is where the heart is.' That doesn't mean that we can't loose our hearts or our focus; doesn't mean the strongest don't have breakdowns. Even superheroes need hugs and pats on the back. We all go out and explore in the world and we make our marks or foot holds so we can find our way back. Sometimes those marks are washed away or fade… or die. Sometimes the scents of our paths seem completely gone. That's when someone comes along, picks up the stray, and gives it a new home, a new mark.

As I stood there watching all of these people helping my husband, I looked over at the concrete patio in front of the boarded back door. Above it was a small cloud of steam from the rain that was still evaporating.

"One, two, three, four, five!" Mouse counted loudly, still sitting in his lap, as her father folded each of her little fingers into a fist.

Sometimes, the things we think we need are washed away, or maybe it's the path we need them on that is washed clean. You decide.

"Crossing bridges into the future requires conquering the past"

Love Anything and Your Heart Will Be Broken
(Precognition)

Dear Angel,
It seems like only yesterday
when we spoke our first hello
We sowed the seeds of love and care
and watched our friendship grow
Together, we braved the bad times
Together, we shared the good
For better and for worse we laughed
and in the storm we stood
And now that we are stars apart
I hope you'll always know
Forever, I will be your friend
Forever, I'll miss you so

It seems like only just last night
the Blue moon shined on us
We vowed our union eternally
from life's dawn till life's dusk
and now that life has taken away
a chance for it to grow,
Forever, I'll remember you
Forever, I'll miss you so

I know the time will come one day
when we will meet again
Then we'll hold on to true love's dream
and never let it end
It'll be just like the way it was,
before the day you left;
before my eyes poured out their tears
each night before I slept
for you're the one who was there

like sunrise, you were true
and no one ever touched my life
as quite the same as you
So whatever the marvels that I will see,
wherever the places I go,
Forever, I'll search to be with you
Forever, I'll love you so.

"Will that be all, Mr. Cole?" The woman behind the cash register impetuously flirted through a crimsoned lips smile which Sean subtly failed to return as she handed back his check card and receipt. Lost in his own uncertainty, he hesitated.

"Yes… thank you… That's all."

The woman's thwarted attempt at socializing showed on her face with a flushing hue of defeat on her cheeks and a frown quickly replacing her pleasant demeanor. Raising her shoulders to herself and with a quick roll of her eyes she shrugged off the rejection and moved on to the next customer.

So deep in thought about the money he was sending to the children and lost in his own hurt, Sean never noticed the rebuff he had dealt the innocent clerk. Thoughts of Shonzé and Alex consumed his mind. It was the first week of December, 2011. In four weeks, Shonzé would be sixteen. In another two months, Alex would be eleven. It had been four weeks since he had seen them, since they had been taken to North Carolina by their grandparents. It had been five weeks since life had taken away their mother, his fiancée. The repeating images of her death crossed his mind again. He had tried hard to ignore them every day since that day. An empty feeling suddenly overwhelmed his stomach, with that feeling itself being replaced just as quickly with his new found anger. *How could she? Why?* Those questions had echoed in his head every hour since the moment he had found out that she had been killed. *She shouldn't have been there!* But she had been and now, now she was gone… forever.

Stepping outside of the Money Union store into the cool fall air, he wondered if their grandmother would even let them know that he sent money to them. She hated him. In his mind, she hated his breath, his thoughts, and the beating of his heart. No matter how deeply from his soul he had tried to love her daughter and those children, Annabelle Stallgood hated him.

Opening the door of his Avalanche and sliding into the driver's seat he wondered if one day, Shonzé and Alex would hate him also. Not for anything he had done but for not being there when they needed him most. But he had no choice. For five years he had been their father but by law of blood he had no say in their grandparents cutting him out of their lives. The curious eyes of Alex were clearly before him. He imagined Alex's pain of never having his real father, losing his mother at this young age, and then losing the only other father he had ever known. And then there was Shonzé. She was about to be sixteen, and in her mind needed no one to help her or tell her anything. She had already been upset at Sean during the past few months. He had tried to start being a firmer parent. And being a strict parent with a know-everything teenager had not gone well. Shonzé made sure as often as possible that he knew how much she disliked his newly enforced strictness. But it was those other times, those barely visible glimpses of love they shared that could never make him stop being the firm father that she needed. They had shared tears through her unreciprocated affection towards teenage boys, through her depressing learning disability in math classes, to overriding her mother's strictness and allowing her to go out with friends and be a teenager; to have some freedom. With hugs for no reasons and every blue moon calling him 'Dad', Shonzé showed that even when she 'hated' him she loved him. But now, would that love be eroded by absence? He wondered would he ever see them or simply talk with them again. *They have a great granddad*, he consoled himself. Forcing a smile to his own face in the rearview mirror, he pulled out of the parking lot and headed home.

December was not as cold as it was empty, not in Georgia, not inside his heart. Remnants of autumn's falling multicolored leaves used to be beautiful. But now, to him, they were like slow motion rain. Sean kept himself busy by working overtime and when he was home he cleaned the house and landscaped the yard over and over. But no matter how much he tried to occupy his mind with other things, the question remained: Why? Why would Angela Stallgood do this to him? Even more than that, the deeper question toyed with him: What did he not do to keep this from happening? It ripped his soul every day to know that those questions would never be answered.

Southern Atlantic Telecom had been his other escape since Angela's death. Working from seven in the morning until beyond quitting time became his normal routine. His gym schedule and nutrition regimen had declined to nonexistent. Sitting on the edge of his bed, his eyes solidly fixed through his window, on the stars of heaven above had become his only pastime. And a broken heart, unable to heal, bled dreams of memories into waking nightmares.

"Hey lil bro. How are you?" the soothing voice of his eternal friend Carol filled his ears through the telephone.

"I'm alright. You know, trying to survive."

"That's all you can do. Survive and grow."

Sean sighed. He loved Carol as if she were his blood sister, but now he did not want to be preached to.

"I was calling to ask if you could swing by the house once or twice a week to check on things. I got selected to go work out of state for a few months."

"Sure. You know I will. What are you going to be doing?"

"Well, you know Southern Atlantic, always downsizing and laying off people, so now they are short on help in Tennessee and are sending a group of Techs to help catch up the workload."

"Oh yeah," Carol laughed sarcastically, "I know, good old Southern A Telecom. They still haven't fixed my high speed internet! And *someone* promised me a month ago to swing by and check my inside wiring."

"I know…I'm sorry," Sean spoke with deep seriousness. "I've been, really distracted…"

"Awww, I'm sorry. I was only joking with you. I know you've had a lot on your plate lately. I would never expect you to be worried about anything else right now. Just get yourself back together. But this trip will be good for you; get away from the familiar areas, get out of your four walls, get some fresh air."

"Yeah," Sean slightly grinned, "it will be good to get away for a minute."

"How long are you gonna be gone?"

"Umm, I'm leaving this Monday, December nineteenth. We should all be coming back at the end of February"

"Dang lil bro! I know you Techs get paid crazy money for working out of town. And for working that long, I'm gonna have to get a loan from you!"

Sean chuckled. Then his smile quickly faded. No matter how much money he made, no amount could ever buy back what he had lost. Time has no price for a heart filled with regret.

"Thanks Carol. You have always been there for me. Thank you so much."

"Hey, cheer up," she ordered, hearing the cracking in his voice. "Just get out of this place, stay busy at work, see some sites, meet some new honeys and let go… Have some fun."

"You know I'm not thinking about being with any women right now. But I will try to stay busy. I…"

"Speaking of which, did u get your black behind back in the gym yet?"

Sean laughed lightly and sighed, "Yeah, yeah. I did some cardio this morning. Felt like I haven't worked out in years."

"That's because you are getting old, old man!"

"If I'm an old man and you are older than me, does that make you, like, uhh, ancient, or…"

"You know what joker?" she snickered. "You best be glad we on the phone right now…"

Sean enjoyed being able to laugh for a moment. It had been his first real laugh since before Angela's death. *Maybe Carol is right*, he contemplated. Maybe it would be good for him to get away from the town, from the places, from the entertainment areas that Angela and he frequented. So close to his relatives and this place having always been his home, he could never leave permanently but he did need to leave it all behind for a while.

Throughout the weekend he cleaned the house, once more, and packed clothes and items he would need for his trip. Along with his work uniforms and a few casual clothes, he included unread books, his story outlines and his laptop. This would be his chance to get away, to rethink, reorganize. Meticulously, Sean planned out each week, with an agenda for each day, things he could do there, like finishing his first book which had been put on hold for so long. By self-examination, the order of his detailed packing, planning, and drive pleased him. He realized he had let so much of himself go over the past five years, sacrificed so much to keep Angela happy, so he thought. But now, noticing that his innate need for structure remained intact, a smile formed on his lips. To him it meant that somewhere in the future, beyond the hurt, past the sleepless nights, there was a definitive glimmer of his original self, his peacefulness, and a life worth living.

Iron John. The book left his hand and seemed to float through the air towards the open suitcase. Not just another unfinished read, but a pathway to his destined peace. And before it landed and clapped against the vinyl folder holding his outlines, a clear image of the bridge sprang into his mind. It had been months since he had been there. The last time, had been with the children, during the past summer. Another memory with them returned to him. This time, the memory included an image of a third child, another boy, another heart embarking on a journey across that bridge. Always philosophical, forever metaphorically observant, he had to go there once more before he left for Tennessee.

Before Sean was completely out of his truck and onto the pavement, a light winter breeze frisked his neck right above the high collar of his wind breaker. Walking through the empty parking lot of Clayton State College, towards the big lake, the half loaf of bread he carried swung freely between his fingers, slapping his right knee sporadically. A distant smell of smoking meat and lighter fluid met him at the top of the hill. One of the families, whose back yard was just beyond the fence at the rear of the lake, was having a Sunday cookout. Mariachi music faintly echoed from inside the house. But as he approached the edge of the big lake, the smells and music disappeared from his senses as the little bridge on the other side of the lake captured his attention. He stood, staring at the bridge which crossed a small expanse between the big lake and a smaller pool of water. Untying the bread, he tore small pieces like he had done many times before and tossed them to the edge of the water. Soon, there were ducks and geese gathering around him, quacking and begging for more. They swam from the farthest part of the lake and they flew in from over the hill where a smaller pond lay. Sean smiled at his old friends. He had forgotten how relaxing it was, to be there, to watch these beautiful birds come up so close. And when the bread was all gone, when the bird's begging had gone unanswered, he turned and looked out at the bridge once more.

In his mind, he saw Shonzé and Alex, with wide eyes, with mouths posed in amazement, dropping crumbs off the side of the bridge into the water as ducks battled fish for every crumb. And beside the two children, in his mind, a third child was there, the one with the fishing rod and big rimmed thick glasses, holding his rod so steady, looking down at the fish waiting for the first catch of his young life. Sean was twelve years old then. Back when Clayton State College was a Junior

College. Before the large campus buildings existed, before the huge dormitories, there was his innocence. Upon that bridge was his beginning. During the summer months, he and friends would ride their bikes to the campus to fish. For a whole summer, he had not caught a single thing. But near the end of summer, on that bridge, from that vantage point, he discovered that he could see right down into the water which was shallow at that end. He could see the fish, the small ones and the large. And on that day, he had dropped a hook baited with a small piece of dough and watched the scene unfold: A medium sized Brim sucked in the bait just as the dough broke the surface of the water, and for a moment, the fish seemed to be motionless and lifeless, perhaps contemplating the realization of its action. That is when Sean's racing heart yanked back his arm and after a brief battle, the fish was out of the water, in his hand, dripping on the bridge. He was almost a teenager. Puberty was already blooming and his voice was already changing. That was the summer he would never forget. But that had been twenty-five years ago. Since then the bridge had been repaired and reinforced. Many fish had been caught. Many moments had been spent there.

As he started towards the bridge, one of those moments stopped him in his tracts. The second most important moment on that bridge had hidden itself deep in his denials. But now, that moment pounced onto his consciousness. A moment with Angela, that should have been his favorite on that bridge, began to claw at his emotions. He could not relive that day. He did not want to remember what happened on that bridge, not now. It was too painful. With that memory, he turned around, clenched his eye lids tightly, slowing but not stopping the streaming tears, and he walked away. He knew the time had to come when he would deal with that recollection, when he would stand on that bridge again, but that moment was somewhere in the future.

They left early in the morning, before sunrise. A convoy of clanging utility vehicles headed north on I-75 towards

Knoxville. With the windows rolled up Sean could still hear the roaring of the diesel engine. He looked forward to getting away, experiencing a new environment. Soon, the local radio station's signals faded into white noise. The second half of his ride he spent tuning the ancient radio to stations that played familiar music. Rarely, did he find that. *This is going to be a long three months*, he thought. And after four hours of travel, including food and restroom breaks, the convoy reached the hotel, nestled across the expressway near the Alcoa airport.

The room he was assigned seemed longer than most. Flipping the light switch at the doorway, the two large full size beds caught his attention first. As Sean drew back the curtain and opened the blinds, the tranquility in the simplicity of the suite relaxed him. As he tossed the first two bags of luggage from the wheeled dolly to on top of one of the beds, the faux mahogany desk and chair caught his eyes. A grin appeared on his lips as he admired the artistic design beveled in the crown molding atop of the built-in cabinet surrounding the desk. This would be his favorite place for the next three months, he determined. He imagined himself laboring late on work nights and through endless hours of his off days, finishing his first book, his first masterpiece that had been put on hold for so long.

Before night had fallen, the desk had been arranged neatly and analytically with his note pads, pens, story folders and his lap top. No familiar surroundings of home to frustrate him. No frequent recreational comforts to distract him. With each moment since his loss of Angela, his determination had been his shepherd and his drive had grown stronger.

Downstairs, the out of town workers of Southern Atlantic Telecom reclined and talked trash to one another as they acquainted themselves with each other since they were all from different work groups. For most, the plan was simple: Work long hours, make an obscene amount of money, and every night drink beer until the A.M. as they sat in the indoor pool and Jacuzzi. Sean laughed inside. To him it was a waste. He knew maybe once or twice within the three months there he would relax in the pool, but he was determined to stay busy, to work diligently in making up for the many years of lost time. During the five years spent with Angela he had rarely worked on his book. Sean had poured himself and buried his thoughts into building her dreams which had become *their* dreams. He reasoned that he would treat her like his queen then and later he would always have time to work on his aspirations. The recollection of this sacrifice angered him slightly. But he immediately knew it had not totally been her fault. Angela had always supported his writing. She had always tried to motivate him, to push him, but her words had often been silenced by her actions. Sometimes, telling him that she was letting him have time to himself to work on his craft in reality meant time away from him in order to venture on her own secret excursions. She was no saint. Still, he accepted and loved her regardless. But his uncertainty of her loyalty always made him feel as if more on his part was needed, as if more labor of love and sacrifice of self was required. He had believed that it was the only way and that through his total focus on her they were becoming stronger, because no matter how rough their many breakups were, she always came back. With a text, a brief call, or a soft knock on his front door, she always returned to him, swearing each time that she had never and could never stop loving him. And he believed that if he waited, if he held on, that one day, they would be strong enough to never part.

Working in East Tennessee was far different from his assignments in the metro areas of Atlanta. The GPS feature of Sean's cell phone became indispensable. The narrow, winding, shoulderless country roads lined with woods and endless glimpses of cows and deer provided long daily episodes of meditation. At times, too long. For in those times, too quiet times, when the unfamiliar radio stations introduced him to new heart palpating melodies, there was nothing and no one to quell the pain of his heart fighting with his memories. Even the familiar songs toyed with him. And when he was beaten down enough by *Love T.K.O* and Joni Mitchell's *See You Sometime*, when his tear ducts could no longer hold back *Could've Been*, he would let it out, letting the secluded country roads conceal his grief. But with each new morning, with each day farther away from the past, he was becoming better; his mind a little clearer.

On Friday morning, December 30th, a second alarm on Sean's cell phone rang loudly as he showered. It was a reminder of Shonzé s birthday, but not that he needed reminding. She and Alex would never be forgotten in his heart.

As he brushed his teeth and buttoned his uniform, he stared at his face in the mirror. He was worn and still stressed. But each day, he was better. Sitting at the edge of the bed, with his cell phone in hand, he smiled as pictures of the kids scrolled before him. Alex with his glasses always at the edge of his nose and Shonzé s huge wide grin, proudly showing her upper gap, always brought him joy. He had to call. They were *his* kids. He had to try. But if their grandmother saw his number she would not answer. Still, he had to try. *Maybe from the hotel phone. Yeah, that's it.* He convinced himself that Annabelle Stallgood would not bother answering a Tennessee number on the caller ID.

After four o'clock, he hoped that both children would be home. Sean made sure that he was back at the hotel early. He smiled with self-commendation when he heard Alex's voice.

"Hello?"

"Hey Alex, how you doing?" he spoke softly.

"Sean!" Alex's cheerful tone squealed in Sean's ears.

"Shhhh! Not so loud! Where's your grandma?"

"Oh yeah," Alex whispered. "She's in the living room, but she has company. Did you remember its Shonzé s birthday? Are you coming to see us?" Alex's questions rattled off quicker than Sean could think of how to answer him.

"Hey little man, slow down. Your grandmother won't let me see yall right now, but maybe in the future we will. Okay? Just always know that I love you and I am always here for you if you need to call me. Okay?"

There was a long silence. Then Alex's cheerful whisper started again.

"Sean, Shonzé said you sent her money for her birthday. Can you send me a Guitar for my birthday? I always wanted one, and you and mommy promised I would have one this year."

Sean's heart rumbled and he refrained from sniffing back the tears.

"Sure little man. I will send you the Guitar. And tell your sister that the money was for both of yall, not just her." The fact that Annabelle had actually let the children know it was from him opened a twinkling of hope. "Now Alex, I need you to go get your sister and put her on the phone but don't let your Grandma know who's on the phone, okay?"

"Okay. Hold on," he whispered.

Sean's heart began to beat loudly as a huge lump formed in his throat. The passing seconds of silence seemed liked minutes. And then, like the dove appearing with the branch, he heard her voice.

"Hello?"

"Hey," Sean hesitated. "Hey baby girl." Another period of silence that seemed to last minutes followed.

"Hey," Shonzé replied somberly.

"How you doing?"

"I'll be okay. Trying to get used to this middle of nowhere life. We are miles away from anything." She was calm. It made him happy that she was still communicating with him. And right before he had become too certain and too hopeful, she fell apart.

"Why did you leave us?" she began to cry.

"What? I didn't leave you. Your grandparents took you away. You know that."

"No, I mean Grandma said that you didn't…" her sniffling and crying became louder. "I asked why we couldn't stay in Georgia and live with you, and Grandma said you didn't want us. Why don't you want us anymore?"

"Baby girl! You know that's not true," his sniffles began. "You know your grandma has always hated me. She's telling you bad things so that you will stop thinking about me and trying to make you forget about me. I want both…"

"You are the only dad I know! I lost mommy and now I don't have you! Why don't you love us anymore?" Her words were barely audible through her crying. And before he could tell her how much he loved her, before he could promise her that her pain would go away some day, the voice he did not need to hear, rattled him through the phone.

"Sean! Is this Sean? Did you dare call my house to upset these kids?" Annabelle Stallgood's raspy voice made his inside curl.

"Annabelle," he said softly, trying to show peace, "I love Shonzé and Alex with all my heart. They are like my own blood. I would never…"

"But they are not your blood! And if it wasn't for you, their mother would still be here!"

"Are you serious? You're blaming me for Angela's death?"

"If you had not been in her life she would not have had to sneak around to be with someone who made her happy! You could never give her happiness! You are broke and have nothing but dreams!"

The coldness in her words heated Sean. Still, he felt that somehow he could get through to her, in order to save his relationship with the children.

"She cheated on *me*, Annabelle," he tried to speak softly. "But she also came back. We broke up many times but we always came back to each other. She loved me for me, not for the money that I didn't have or may never have. She knew that I would provide and protect and love her and the children with my life. She…"

"N-n-n-no! N-n-n-no! She knew better! That's why she cheated on you! You have nothing and will never be nothing! She was not happy with you! And you are not going to take the happiness away from these kids. Don't call them ever again! And if you call this house again, I will get a restraining order!"

There was a loud click followed by returning dial tone. As he sat at the side of the bed, staring at the phone, self-doubt began to creep into his thoughts. Was Annabelle right? Had Angela been miserable? But why had she stayed in the relationship with him? Would he ever know? Would he ever see the children again? For the hour that followed, he could only sit and question without answering. And when the hour passed, the hotel phone still lay clutched in his hand and his heart still lay broken in two. That's when the song, another new song from the unfamiliar radio station heard earlier that day, began to play clearly in his head. It was the acoustic version of Katy Perry's *The One That Got Away.* Scrolling through his phone pictures again, the rosined bow softly kissing strings of a cello stabbed at him. Tracing the curve of Angela's smile, the melody tore his soul. Zooming in on her hazel eyes set in a back drop of her light honey skin, the singer's voice all but destroyed his spirit. In two nights it would be a new year; the time for most to start over. *In another life*, he repeated the lyrics, *I would make you stay…*

January came with light coldness and heavy loneliness. Sean had spent many hours tapping on the keys of his laptop. The moments in between had been filled with fending off memories he still was not ready to confront.

Against his original plans he spent more than a couple of days hanging out with his co-workers at the pool and Jacuzzi. But he still refused to drink alcohol or stay out late. His core of direction was still intact. He even began working out again in the hotel gym. Being away from home, talking bull with other guys, beginning to notice other women again, was helping him begin to feel happiness anew. But watching the escapades of a few married co-workers who hooked up with women they met there, angered him. Yet, somewhere, in his broken hearted mind, he started to accept, *that* was a part of the world he lived in.

The end of January brought his thirty-eighth birthday. "Headed for the big Four-O!" the guys he worked with all chimed the morning of. The entire week was filled with his co-workers taking him out for dinner, alerting every restaurant of the occasion in order to get free drinks or desserts. And when February came, beginning to feel happier and starting to let go of his past, he did not forget Alex's request. Sean made sure an electric guitar was shipped to Alex. No matter how much of the past he would someday let go of, he could never let go of his children.

Near the last week of February, almost at the end of his out of town assignment, his longing for home began to strain him. Although he had spent time at restaurants with co-workers and meeting the strange and interesting deep woods customers of the Tennessee Mountains, and even with the large amount of progress made towards the completion of his book, he longed for nothing more than the comfort of his own bed. On a restless Tuesday evening, breaking routine of writing and exercise, he dressed in jeans and a black sweater layered beneath a thick leather coat. Purposely missing the usual group of co-workers who hung out at sports bars and the indoor pool in the evenings, he waited for the hotel shuttle.

"You by yourself tonight sir?" inquired the driver.

"Yeah. Just me. I want to go somewhere different. Any suggestions?"

"Whew, I don't know. You boys have hit just about every restaurant and bar within my driving range."

Sean sat quiet for a moment, thinking as he listened to the low rumble of the passenger van. "What about out of your driving range?"

"Well, I know a place that has really great food, but officially, I can't take you that far."

Sean smirked as he leaned to the side and reached into his right pocket, pulling out a wad of cash. Then he fastened his seatbelt and laid fifty dollars over the shoulder of the driver. "We'll just keep this 'unofficial' then."

O'Grady's was an upscale restaurant closer towards the west side of Tennessee, about thirty minutes from the hotel. With his black leather loafers, dark black denim jeans, and cotton turtleneck sweater, Sean appeared not to be too underdressed. Walking in without a date, he felt awkward sitting alone at a table surrounded by almost formal wearing up tights so he opted to sit at the bar instead. Not noticing the bar tender, he slid into the bar stool backwards while admiring the restaurants décor.

"Welcome to O'Grady's. What can I get you to drink?"

The voice was alien to his ears yet welcoming. Swinging around in his seat, his confident composure was caught off guard by the gorgeous woman smiling from behind the bar.

"Umm, yeah, I…I want, a, umm…"

"We don't serve any of that," she joked. "But I can get you a beer."

Sean chuckled, dropping his head, recomposing himself, then looked back at her with a smile. "I'm sorry, It's just, that..." *that you are drop dead gorgeous*, he wanted to say. "That, I'm new around here and I'm just trying to check out my surroundings."

"Well, no matter where you're from, I'm sure I have a drink that will make you feel at home." Her smile never faltered as she talked. And her sultry dark eyes never left his.

"I don't really drink. But I would like a club soda, or lemonade."

"Awww, no alcohol," she playfully pouted her bottom lip. "I can tell that you work out. Is it a diet thing?"

"No. I'm just always working on some project or thinking about working on something that involves my unaltered mind… Ever since I was a kid I was always building or designing something. Just kind of always been afraid of losing or altering that creativity, you know?"

"Hmmm. I sense a little bit of control freak there… Like you always want or plan things to be exactly a certain way."

Sean smiled as he turned away from her with a light blush then back with a guilty gaze into her eyes.

"Yeah," she nodded. "I get that. I'm an artist, well, aspiring artist. When I am creating, I need my full mental capacity. But come on, you're not always *working* are you? What type of job do you do?" As her eyes stayed locked onto his, her hands whipped, poured, and slid drinks to opposite sides of the counter like a rehearsed choreographed routine.

"I work for S-A-T. We're here, up from Georgia, helping out with the work load. But when I'm not working there I'm working on my writing career, always thinking or seeing something that could be a story."

"Really? I love to read. I think that writing is kind of like art. It's creative and explorative. Have you published anything yet?"

Sean smiled. He felt so much comfort sitting there, looking at her. Besides Carol, he had spoken to no one about his book during the past three months. "I'm working on my first now. I hope to have it finished by the end of this year."

"Awesome! What's your name, so I'll know who to look for?"

"Sean. Sean Cole." He beamed. "And what's the name of the artist that I need to look for?"
"Raven, Topeland."

"Raven. That's nice. I'd love to see some of your work."

She blushed and quickly glimpsed across the restaurant toward the kitchen entrance.

"Tell you what. Let me get your order in and when I get a moment I'll get my cell out of the back; I have a few pics on it."

"That's cool. What's good here?"

"Everything. But the steak is the best!"

For a moment, he lost himself, staring across at her creamed caramel skin, admiring her long jet black silky hair and large coffee bean colored eyes.

"Well," he grinned subtly, "that's what I want, the best."

Sean spent the rest of the evening talking to her. She spent almost all of her time in front of him, somewhat neglecting the other patrons. And throughout the night he found, by scrolling through her cell phone pictures, that she was more than an *aspiring* artist. She was at an artistic level beyond professional, beyond working there, behind a bar in a small country town. And for the first time, in years, his mind was actually fixated with a woman other than Angela. It felt good though strange. As even more time passed, would he forget her? He did not want to. He longed for the hurt to leave completely but he never wanted to stop loving her. To love Angela had been his food, his purpose. Once, in 2009, Angela had sent him a news clip from weirdasianews.com about a man whose wife had died. The man loved her so much he had entombed her dead body with clay in their house where each night he slept beside her, holding her, for five years. At that time, Sean had thought it was the most insane thing that he had read. But now with his heart, his breath no longer there, he understood.

"Aw man," he noticed the time on his cell phone.

"What's wrong?" Raven asked.

"It's ten thirty. I have to call the shuttle guy to pick me up before his cut off time."

"Well, I enjoyed talking with you. Maybe you can come back and see me sometime."

He contemplated the invitation. His natural male mentality bowed to the proposal but his analytical mind questioned his readiness. "I think I can do that," he surrendered, his polished grin flirting back at her.

"Well here's my number," she offered, scribbling on the back of his receipt. "In case, you know, you get lost and forget where I am."

"I seriously doubt that I will forget you," he assured.

Raven left him as he placed his call to the shuttle driver. Sean basked in the emotions he was experiencing, feelings not felt since his life with Angela, which for a moment, seemed a long time ago. But on his ride back to the hotel, he realized that it was not long ago. He missed Angela as if it were yesterday. He still felt anger about the way she died, he still felt frustrated when he thought of that day at the bridge, and he still felt pain after dreaming of being with her, only to awaken in the hotel bed to the reality that she was gone. But no matter how much his emotions vacillated from anger to sadness, he never wanted to let go of loving her.

Passage of time slowed during the following two days. Sean was exhausted from working long hours during the day while tolling over his book late into the night. Endless meals from restaurants and hotel catering had become mundane. And now a new distraction, in the form of a five foot four beauty, had taken a small yet forceful hold of him. *Too soon*, he thought. Too soon after Angela, it could only end in hurt for the innocent beautiful bartender. Still, he found himself there once more, perched upon the bar stool grinning at her welcoming face.

"Hey you," she smiled.

"You remember me?" he tested.

"Of course... Mr. Soon to be Published! Why would I forget you?"

There was a difference about Raven that he noticed. This night, her smiles seemed forced. From the moment he walked in, she had been constantly checking her cell phone. Conversation with her was shorter than before, however, she still spent more time with Sean than with the other patrons.

"What's wrong," he searched.

"Nothing. Why do you ask?"

"You seem distant."

A heavy sigh preceded a halfhearted grin on her face. "Just boyfriend problems, nothing new."

"I can understand that, believe me."

"You having girl problems too?"

"No. Had. We used to have rocky times but things were starting to get better and then… then they didn't."

Raven ceased her multitasking and was standing still, compassionately staring at him. The anger that had appeared and abated back and forth since Angela's death, now cloaked his face. It had come so suddenly that he never noticed his rising pulse or the tightening of his lips.

"Hey… you okay?" Raven inquired, reaching across the counter, rubbing the back of his hand. The softness of her touch, a woman's touch, not felt for so long, quickly broke him from his quiet rage.

"Yeah, yeah, I'm good. Just, it was just… well it ended badly."

"You want to talk about it?"

Sean, turned his head, then back to her. "You know, you had me talking up a storm the other night. You bartenders are good at that, huh? Well how about I play 'bartender' tonight, and you do the talking? Tell me the trouble you're having."

Raven blushed and gave way to a smile, a real smile, and slid two glasses toward the end of the bar.

"Ok, we can do that. The short story: I fell in love with a selfish jerk. I dropped out of art school and moved out here with him because he said we had better opportunity here. Turns out, it was better opportunity for him to get deeper into his meth dealing and more time for his video games. And so here I am, stuck here after four years, turning twenty-eight soon, with nothing to show for it."

"Wow. Sorry to hear that. Where did you move from?"

"Chicago, Tri-Taylor. Born and raised. My mother and father live there still. It's my dad's home town. My mom is from Korea; he met her while he was stationed there and when he retired they settled back in Illinois. I actually have an older sister who lives near you, in Georgia. She's been trying for the longest to get me to come live with her so I can go back to school. It's just hard... leaving. I love him, but I know he's no good for me." Raven's eyes seemed to narrow as she stared for a moment at the beer dispenser, one hand resting on the tap. "He enjoys playing those stupid games more than spending time with me. Can you believe that? I don't even know why I stay."

The cheer filled beautiful lady he had met nights before, no longer existed. Now, unable to force a smile, Raven excused herself and disappeared through the kitchen doors. Sean's empathy reached out and felt the tremors of her spirit. He knew all too well her pain. *Why do we stay? Is it love that makes us hope or hope that makes us love?* Sitting at the empty bar, staring up at the large screen monitors which showed highlights of the night's games, he reflected over the years spent with Angela. So many disagreements, so many break ups. Had it been worth it? Was there a purpose?

Soon, Raven had reappeared behind the counter.

"You cool?" He asked softly.

"Yeah, I'm good." Her cheerful tone had returned. "Just fed up, you know?"

"Yeah, I know. I understand"

The rest of the night was spent unanimously on subjects that did not deal with sour relationships. They discussed their hobbies, their family, and friends. They revealed their passions and pet peeves. The minutes on the clock ran like water through a stream, and before they realized, it was twelve a.m.

"Damn. Guess I have to call a cab." he lamented.

"Why?" Raven's curious gaze taunted him.

"Hello? Shuttle? It's after his quitting time. Remember?"

"Hello! Smart ass! I have a car!" she chided. "I'll be off in an hour."

"You're gonna give me a ride? It's thirty minutes away from here and you said you live in the opposite…"

"Sean," she cut him off, staring at him with eyes mantled in pain, her spirit in need of solace, "I really don't want to go home now."

The thirty minute drive was cut down to a little more than fifteen minutes by Raven's heavy foot. Sitting beside her, Sean glanced around to the back seat, surveying the hoard of art brushes, paint, oil, and a pair of elegant high heels.

"Don't judge me," she smiled, noticing his wondering eyes. "I'm always on the go."

"So you still paint?"

"Never stopped. I left art school, but I can't leave art. That's in my blood."

With another glance, a pile of clothes in the rear of her SUV caught his attention.

"You need to do your laundry?"

"Oh my god!" Raven grinned and blushed. "Get out of my business, man! I don't always stay at home." Her smile quickly faded. "It's not always a happy place."

"I'm sorry," he sighed. "Why don't you just…" Catching himself with a portent of the morsel of his own foot stuck in his mouth, he turned and watched the bright highway lights zooming by.

The ride to the hotel was mostly in silence. A long day's fatigue and soft music from the radio accounted for their lack of conversation. But when her little SUV whipped into the parking lot, instead of dropping him off at the front door she pulled into a parking space and turned off the engine. Staring at him, through the darkness between them, her beauty aroused him but her sadness kept him at bay.

"Sooooo, what are you going to do when you go in?" Raven asked.

"I don't know, maybe play cards with the guys, or work on my book, or maybe… I don't know."

"Sooooo, can I come play cards with you?"

Sean sighed silently. "Raven, do you want to come upstairs?"

"Yes," she nodded, her large coffee bean eyes sparkling from the light of a passing car.

Why not, he looked away, rolling his eyes.

Opening the hotel room door, Sean noticed his work boots and dirty uniform strewn out on the floor. Quickly grabbing them, he threw them across the room to the side of the bed on the far end on the suite. When he turned around, Raven stood, with a huge grin plastered on her face. "I see I'm not the only one who's on the go."

When Sean stepped out of the bathroom, after brushing his teeth, he found Raven lying across the bed, flipping through the television remote, with the deck of cards from the desk now on the bed in front of her.

"So what are we playing?" she perked.

"Well, the guys are all at the pool or knocked out, and the only game I know for two people is the one my ex taught me."

"Gee, great," she sighed.

"You'll like it."

"Okay, but if I'm going to let you show me this, you have to be honest with me. What's up with you and the ex? You hoping to get back with her?"

Sean smiled disconcertedly as he sat down and shuffled the cards on the bed.

"Naww, I don't think that will ever be possible… she died in November."

"Oh, I'm so sorry. I didn't know."

"It's cool. I'm just trying to get on with life."

"That's what you meant when you said things were starting to get better and then they didn't?"

"Yeah," he chuckled. "There's a little more to it though." As he shuffled and dealt the cards, he noticed Raven's questioning stare. "She, cheated, I guess."

"You guess?"

"You know how it is, when I first got a hint of something, or looking back now, there were times when she was in the shower with her cell phone on top of the shower or hidden in her jeans balled up on the floor."

"O-o-o-oh, the cell phone thing. Yeah, been there, done that."

"And then, times when I would come around the corner and she would abruptly get off the phone. And finally, I saw her cell phone bill and when I went through it, there was a long history of calls, late nights, early mornings, or other times when she was away from me. Found out that it was a guy, this guy named Matt, who lived near her neighborhood. It was a big blow up. But we worked it out. She still never admitted to it. Tried to make me believe it was about business." He laughed to himself. "We went back and forth with this, you know. I never understood why she kept cheating or breaking up with me, but then she would always come back. I told her a hundred times if she wasn't happy to go. But she would go and always come back."

Sean's eyes were filled with tears about to fall when Raven's fingers rubbed against his cheeks halting their decent, urging him to sniff them away.

"I'm sorry," he pulled back. "I just never loved someone so much. Just don't understand why she would keep coming back if she didn't really want to be with me."

"So, when she died, how was the relationship?"

Sean sarcastically laughed out loud, clutching his stomach as if he could not bear the humor in the question.

"Before she died, we had gotten engaged. We were working on getting our finances and credit in better condition. We shared almost everything, so I thought. She was great at helping me manage my debt and save. And she led me to believe that she was getting her debt paid off and we were helping each other with financial problems that came up. We went everywhere together. We took small inexpensive trips and vacations with the kids. We were a family. After we got engaged, I moved in and things were better. She showed so much attention to me, I was never able to call her first cause she called me all day and every day. So when I found out the last time that she was cheating again, it completely caught me off guard."

"How did you find out that time?"

With a tight lump in his throat and failure to fight back a falling tear, he stood up from the bed and turned away toward the window. "When she died, she was killed in a car wreck. She was in his car, with him... with Matt."

Turning back around at the sound of the bed movement, he caught her hands reaching up to hug him and softly pushed them back down to her side.

"It's okay, I'm okay," he smiled. "She died and… he died. But the question of why she did what she did is still here."

Raven gazed at him, unable to find empathetic words. He could tell, by the vexation in her face that her current relationship echoed similar sentiments.

"Don't get me wrong. I'm no saint," he added. "I used to be a player. Not on purpose, but I had many female *friends*; Things happened. But when I met her and the kids, that all stopped. I never cheated on her! She was my everything!" He shook his head and stared at the floor. "I keep wondering if it was karma for me; her cheating." A lump swelled in his throat again. "Still, I wish, even if she had left me to be with him permanently, I wish that she had never died. I, I just wish she was still here, alive and happy…At least alive, there would still be a chance for us… or a chance for me to understand why… But dead?" he shook his head and clenched his teeth tightly. "I can't fight death."

With her hands now free from Sean's restraint, Raven reached up quickly, pulling his tall frame down and locking around his neck in a tight embrace.

"It's okay," she whispered. "You are going to be fine. It just takes time."

This time, Sean did not push away. He needed the consoling. He needed a shoulder. But he also realized he needed a limit. Holding her felt good, too good, too strange. Almost as quickly as she had embraced him he just as quickly interrupted the bond, slowly removing her hands from around him. As they let go of one another, the book on the night stand caught Raven's eye.

"What's that about?"

"Iron John? It's, it's kind of like modern mythology. It's about men going through a rite of passage from boy to manhood. I just finished it, finally. It's one of my favorites."

"Why is that?"

"It reminds me of my life with Angel, my ex. Her name was Angela, but I always called her Angel. She was... my Angel."

"Awww, that's so sweet."

Sean sighed. "Every time I see that book, I remember this stupid bridge... It's bitter sweet."

"Bridge? What bridge?" she yawned.

A long pause succeeded. As he stepped around her and sat down on the bed again, she followed. In silence, she pulled a pillow to her side, lay down on it, and awaited his reply.

"It's just one of those things, those moments between us. I have questions but will never know the answers."

"Tell me," Raven mumbled, her cheek pressing against the pillow, with hair draped across her face.

For a moment he ceased shuffling the cards. Looking away from her toward the muted television, he began to realize his embarrassment of crying in front of her earlier. *It's too much for one night. She didn't come here to hear sad stories,* he thought. Turning back to her, he saw that her eyes had completely closed and her mouth was hanging slightly open against the pillow.

"Raven?"

"Uh huh," she muttered.

Smiling, he gathered the cards and placed them on the nightstand then clicked off the television.

"Hey?" he said, pulling back the covers. "Slide up here."

Half asleep, with Sean's help, she crawled underneath the sheets, righting herself on the pillow against the headboard.

"Tell me," Raven mumbled again, her eyes still closed, "bout the bridge."

Turning off the lamp on the night stand, he pulled the comforter snuggly over her shoulder up to her neck.

"Another time," he murmured.

Moving his suit case and carefully arranged folders to the floor and off of the second bed, he pulled back the sheet and comforter. Sean sat down on the bed, perching his heels up on the wooden ridge that edged the box spring. Staring through the dark at her as she faintly snored, his thoughts were months away. After minutes of reminiscing about the past, he lay down on his side, and continued staring across the room at Raven. *Wonder if I'm going to wake up with all my stuff stolen?* he teased himself. *Or wake up dead?* He smiled and closed his eyes. But somewhere, between the middle of night and the breaking of dawn, he awoke, with Raven's diminutive snoring no longer far away, but right next to him. With her head nuzzled on the side of his chest and her arm across his torso he could feel the slow beating of her heart even through the clothes they both slept in. Deeply inhaling the conditioned scent of her black strands sprawled beneath his chin, a smile made its way to his lips and he closed his eyes and dozed off again.

When morning came, Sean awoke with his back turned toward her. Raven's arm lay hooked around his midsection. Still in their clothes from the night before, along with their connecting body heat, they both had sweated fiercely during their sleep. He slid out of bed slowly, attempting not to wake her, and lowered the thermostat. As he groomed, showered, and got ready for work, he checked on her often. Raven's snoring had faded, but he could tell she was in a deep sleep and greatly exhausted. Preparing to walk out of the door, he tried to wake her.

"Raven?" he spoke softly. "Hey you?"

Other than the visible rise and falling of her chest, she remained motionless. He wrote a note and tucked it half way into her purse, which still rested on top of the other bed:

Good morning. I had to go to work. I tried to wake you. They serve free breakfast downstairs until 10. Here's a room key card. You can stay as long as you like. Thanks for listening last night. I owe you a card game.
Sean

Closing the room door, he stood for a second outside in the hall. The company laptop swinging from the shoulder strap booted up with a series of beeps. He had begun logging in before walking out of the hotel room. After a few seconds of gathering his senses, he turned around, slid his card in the door slot and reentered the room. Walking past her, he took his personal laptop from the desk and quietly slid it into his back pack. Before exiting the room again, he turned back and smiled at the sleeping beauty. *You're fine, but I'm not that crazy.*

During the day, he called her cell to check on her. She never answered. When he returned that evening, she was gone. His second room card and a folded note lay on top of the bed:

Thank you for letting me have a getaway last night. You have no idea how much that relaxed me. Have to go home and deal with his mouth today and I have to work tonight. I'll call you. Take care,
Rae

A day passed and he still had not heard from her. Had her boyfriend confronted and hurt her, or had Sean's preoccupation with his past scared her away? Wondering if he would ever see her or hear from her again, he began preparing for his trip home. It was Saturday, and on the following Thursday, he and his co-workers would be heading back to Georgia. Taking advantage of the remaining time he had away from his normal surroundings, he spent Saturday evening working heavily on his book. So focused, so mentally worked, the ringing of his cell phone brought a welcomed surprise.

"Hello?"

"Hey," came Raven's chipper voice. "Whatcha doing?"

"Hey. I'm just here, in my room, not doing much?"

"Oh. I'm at work, so I can't talk long. Just was wondering if you would like to go somewhere tomorrow, or do you have to work?"

"No, I mean, yeah, I would like to go somewhere," he laughed. "No, I don't have to work."

"I'll pick you up around seven, and we can get breakfast, if that's okay with you?"

"You are welcome to stay here again and we could wake up and have breakfast," he gleamed.

Raven laughed softly. "I really shouldn't have done that. I want to apologize. I was too forward. It's just been really hard at home lately."

"No, it's cool. What did he say about you not coming home?"

"Um, he… it doesn't matter. I'm surprised he even noticed. No big deal though."

"Are you okay?"

"Yeah. I'm fine," she said in hurried tone. "Just be ready in the morning, alright? I have to get back to the bar. See ya."

With the click of the phone, Sean entertained the idea of spending time with her, yet he worried about the drama she faced at home. He reasoned that she needed him to escape her present just as she had been his temporary refuge from his past. *Was it right or wrong for either of them?* At that moment he did not care.

The next morning, dressed in his jeans and running shoes with a cotton pullover, he admired her apparel when she walked into the lobby. With her pink hoodie, fitted jeans and hiking boots, they were a cute couple. Both laughed and talked through their meal at the small breakfast bar not far from the hotel.

"Where you taking me?" he asked as her SUV rolled down the expressway.

"The Lost Sea!" she sang. I've lived here all this time and never been. Always wanted to go but *he* never had time."

Sean's face grew cold. Immediately, thoughts of Angela's secret rendezvous with Matt entered his mind. *Was this the way it happened, he thought.* He had tried any and every activity, restaurant, and exploration that Angela had asked of him. Still, something had escaped his notice, he reasoned – *why else would she have hung out in secret with another man.*

"And you did ask him?" he questioned.

"Yeah, many times. Tried to surprise him and he still wouldn't go." Noticing his pleasant demeanor had been replaced with a stern one, she frowned as she glanced at him and back towards the road. "Why'd you ask that?"

"Just wondering… And, it's funny… my ex and I brought the kids here, to Tennessee last summer. We went to Gatlinburg and planned to come back this year. The Lost Sea was one of the places we were gonna go. Just funny, that's all."

"Oh. Well, do you want to go somewhere different?"

"No. I'm sorry. I don't mean to bring her up again. I just remembered, that's all. I really want to go. And I know that you want to really bad. So let's go. Let's do this!"

Raven accepted his words with a smile. However, as they continued their conversation and made the drive, his brief moments of self-questioning did not go unnoticed. Even during the Lost Sea tour, mixed in with their laughs and enjoyment were the repeated instances where Sean appeared divided from the present.

In a large cavern, the group of tourist admired the ridged formations and crystal clusters which hung from the ceiling. Raven reveled in finally seeing nature's hidden artwork. She could not stop smiling. Noticing that Sean was no longer right beside her, she broke away from the others and found him a few yards behind. He was standing at a point of the path, which flanked on both sides by wooden guard rails and jutted out over a small expanse, looked like a tiny bridge. He was holding on to the rail, looking over and down into the sand.

"Hey. You trying to loose me," she said, slipping her arms around him from the side.

"No," he smiled. "Of course not."

"What do you see down there?"

"Nothing. Just reminds me of another place."

Taking his right hand in her left palm, she stroked his wrist.

"I've been thinking about what you said the other night. You wondered why your ex would keep breaking up with you or cheat but keep coming back to be with you."

"Yeah?" he growled, barely audible to her.

"It's because she was in love with you, Sean. Even though she wanted other things or thought she wanted to try other things or other people, she probably was struggling with herself and could never let go of you because she never stopped being in love with you."

In his heart he wanted to believe this. But in his mind, filling again with the fluctuating anger he had for Angela, there still existed the feeling of unreasonable injustice.

"How would *you* know?" he spoke coldly.

His bitter words tore Raven's hands away from his, and her sympathetic eyes followed, as she turned and headed back toward the rest of the group. "Raven, I'm sorry!" he yelled. *Nice Sean, real nice.*

The remainder of the tour was spent in silence between the two. Raven exchanged half smiles of courteousness for his apologetic gazes. Any extra plans for the rest of the day certainly had been cut short by his insensitivity. When she pulled up to his hotel, Raven hugged him tightly before he stepped out of her SUV. And without a goodbye, without a response to his farewell, she sped away.

The days that followed returned him to the emptiness which he had brought with him to Tennessee. Sean's calls and texts to Raven went unanswered. Unaware of the extent in hurt he caused, he decided against visiting her at *O'Grady's*. And when he left for Georgia, on that cool Thursday morning, he took her with him in his mind, and hoped to see her again.

****

"Hey lil' bro. How was Tennessee?" Carol inquired.

"It was… interesting. Just got back a week ago."

"If you're calling about the stories you sent for me to proofread, I read two. *Rain Dogs* and *No Such Thing as Monsters*."

"Ok. Wasn't calling about that, but what do you think so far?"

"I absolutely love *Rain Dogs*. I like *No Such Thing*, but what's the deal with the stoic style of writing? It doesn't have your usual poetic flare."

"I was always taught not to use beautiful words to describe ugly things."

"Hmmm, okay."

"But I didn't call to discuss the book," he pressed.

"What is it?"

"I met someone there."

Carol laughed loudly. "Oh you found you a mountain hillbilly girl and got you a piece of..."

"No, crazy! She lives there, but she definitely is not from there. But we hit it off. And no, I did not sleep with her!"

"So this is serious? Do you really think you are ready for this, so soon?"

"Don't worry, we are not starting anything. Haven't heard from her since I been back. But I think that we will end up being good friends... I hope."

"So what's bothering you about it?"

"Just… I don't know. I guess wanting to have something with her but knowing I'm not over Angela yet."

"You don't need me to tell you that. You know if you get with this girl, she'll be like a rebound to you and when you finally let go of Angela, she might get hurt... Maybe you should just not even be friends with her. I know that sounds harsh but you know what I'm saying. It would be best... for both of you."

"I know," he uttered with reluctance. "I know."

"Besides," she added, "finishing this book is probably great therapy for you. Helps you reboot your mind and helps you let go of your past worries; Gives you something fresh and new to focus on."

"Really?" he asked in a deep sarcastic tone. "Is that what this book is supposed to do, get me over Angela? Well I will be glad when that day gets here, 'cause it sure is taking its time."

"But that's what it takes, time."

Dropping the phone's mouth piece down, he gave a long sigh.

"It gets better after a while," she continued, "I promise... And besides, you don't have time to sulk. You need to be out shopping for clothes for my wedding! Did you R.S.V.P. me back on the email invite?"

"No. Other than the stories I emailed you from Tennessee I haven't read my emails. I think my inbox is packed. What do I need, a tux?"

"No, muscle brains. Read your email. It's a White Party Wedding; everyone is wearing white. We're going to exchange our vows and then party through the night. No kids, no one under twenty-one, and there will be plenty of food and yes, kiddo, you are having a glass of wine with me and a dance!"

"Wow," he chuckled. "This is a new one. I don't think I have any white dressy clothes."

"Well, get some. And open your dang email! I need you to R.S.V.P. that invite for the caterer."

"Alright, alright, I will."

The days became weeks, leaving the coldness of the past. With each sunrise, came stronger focus. Workouts increased in consistency, and the quality of his writing progressed. The pieces of dreams, stunted so many years ago, began to mend themselves. And though pain was beginning to submit to time, the frustration and anger still refused to relinquish their reign. *Why*, visited him daily. *Why*, became his nemesis.

Days before the wedding, Sean found himself at D&K clothing, his final stop on a long day of disappointing searches for apparel. Trying on white wing tip shoes, and white linen pants and shirt in the dressing room, he smiled in the mirror. The entire ensemble fit his toned form perfectly. He chuckled to himself, as he unclasped the top two buttons of the shirt, revealing the defined cleft between his pectoral muscles. He thought of how Angela used to slide her fingers across his collar bone and down across his chest whenever she helped straighten his collar. He remembered how it was Angela who had always picked out his clothes. Had she been there, he would never have spent so much of the day searching for clothes to fit his not so average build. She knew every inch of him. She knew what fit and what made him handsome. She would be so proud of him, he imagined. His smile shinning back at him in the mirror was real; a smile which was a lasting fragment of the happiness she had constructed inside of him. *You look so good*, he imagined her saying. His body was back to the form he had before she had passed, before depression had smothered his will. He had worked so hard in the gym. He also had worked intensely on his mind. Sticking to his agenda of working long hours on his book and his spiritual soul searching, his drive and his motivation had grown stronger, deeper, and better.

"Sean?" a familiar voice questioned as he stepped out from the dressing room.

"Hey!" he said, as he turned, his eyes meeting Mrs. Maleatha, Angela's hair dresser. "How are you?"

Reaching up and hugging him tightly. "I'm good. Are you okay?"

"Yeah. I'm great," he lied.

"I haven't seen you since last year, since... the funeral. You haven't been by to see me."

"Well," he looked away, as memories began to surface, "you know, not many reasons to see you on Sundays anymore. I mean, you know, I love you like family, but no need for those Sunday visits." He thought of how Angela used to have her hair fixed every Sunday afternoon in the small home basement shop of Mrs. Maleatha. He would sit, no matter how long, talking with her and her husband Patrick while the kids played video games or entertained themselves, while she worked on Angela's hair. It had been another place that he and Angela shared together. Another place filled with memories which he had avoided ever since her death.

"You don't have to come on Sundays, baby. We always home. The boys moved back home, so somebody's always there. What you doin up here?"

"Uh, just getting some clothes to go to a friend's wedding," he said cutting his eyes to the folded garments on the hanger over his shoulder.

Reaching out and rubbing the fabric between her fingers, she smiled in approval. "I bet that looks good on you. Angela always loved shopping for you. She loved to dress her man." Her smiling lips began to clinch tight as tears formed in her eyes.

"Don't you start," he said, pulling her back to him in an embrace.

"She loved you so much," she muttered against his chest.

Sean wanted to respond. But he could not. For the moment, for the day, he was at peace. Mrs. Maleatha had never known about the relationship between Angela and the other man. She had only been aware of the many breakups and the numerous makeups between the two. She had only seen akin affections and actions between Angela and Sean.

"Whew," she smiled, letting go of his hug. "No matter how many times y'all broke up, y'all always came back together. She would have never left you, baby. After y'all got engaged, it was like y'all were already married. It was like she was your wife and you were her husband. Y'all were a family!" She sniffed and wiped her wrist across her eyes. "She was your wife, baby. I'm so sorry it happened. I know you miss her. We miss her too."

Sean only nodded. He felt empathy for Mrs. Maleatha's pain. But minute anger at her words kept his tears away.

"Yeah," he consoled. "It's gotten better. It'll be better as time goes by. At least, that's what everyone tells me." *But does the anger ever go?* He wondered. *Will I ever find the answers to 'why'?*

Some things, no matter how small, can bring down the largest mountains. Like the stone to Goliath, like the spurs to a trot, we are all simple… we are all of clay.

Spring brought life to nature and with it, a warm April Saturday. The banquet hall at the Hyatt was decorated with soft white table cloths, place settings, and light blue truffle accents and arrangements throughout. Sitting at a table with wedding guest he did not know, Sean fondled with and admired the personalized wine glass placed before each guest. *Michael and Carol, April 21, 2012.* Large silver stars hung in various spaces across the hall's ceiling. Far removed from his own worries, he enjoyed every moment, every smiling face. And just before the wedding began, a woman, wearing a short, fitted white skirt and low cut, white, shoulder strapped top, entered the room. As she made her way across the room, to take a seat at the table in front of Sean's, her attractiveness did not go undetected. From the tips of her silver and white stilettos to the ends of her golden hued hair, every eye in the room noticed her. Before she took her seat, only a yard in front of him, she glanced back at

Sean. Her long dainty eye lashes baited him, her fire pink lips pursed into a smile.

He gulped.

The wedding party, climaxing with the freshly shaved groom, entered the hall. They each wore all white with the groom's handkerchief a turquoise blue. And when all had settled, when anticipation had peaked, Carol, entered the hall, the radiance of her moment shining in her smile. With light blue eye shadow and a turquoise ruffled strapless dress, she and Michael looked amazing.

"…Yeah, I dressed him; made us match," she joked later in the ceremony.

Sean was happy to be there, everyone was. But through the joy, amid the countless attractive faces, the woman with the fire pink lips stayed on his mind. A barrage of male admirers took their turns swinging their lines, one by one striking out. With each rejection, Sean took note and contemplated a different technique. But one patron, skilled in charisma, successfully encouraged the woman to the dance floor. As Sean sat barely sipping the wine, regretting his hesitation of approach, Carol, grabbed and squeezed him in a hug from behind.

"You made it!" she screamed. "Look at you! You so damn sexy!"

"Really," he grinned turning to embrace her, "you checking me out at your wedding?"

"Umph! I might have to get it annulled," she teased.

"Dang you crazy. Does Mike know how crazy you are? You look so beautiful! Congratulations."

"Yeah, we finally did it. We are finally here. And I see somebody's trying to drink with the adults tonight," she said, tapping her nails on his wine glass.

"Yeah, I think I'm getting buzzed already."

"Rookie! Don't you come up in here and get drunk at my wedding. I'll have to worry about one of these hoochies trying to take you home."

"Speaking of that," he motioned with his head toward the attractive woman still dancing on the floor, "do you know her? Or does, Mike, or anybody…"

"I know her," she rolled her eyes, then erased her smile with a serious stare. "But the answer is no."

"What? Ah c'mon, I need some leverage, some inside info. Every guy here is…"

"No. Sean, you are like the brother I never had, and I love your friendship deeper than you could know. But look at her Sean."

"I did," he smirked. "Been doing that all evening." He raised his glass up to his lips as he turned to stare at the woman again.

"Look," she said, taking the glass from his hands. "Come with me."

Smiling and greeting the guests as she walked through the crowd, Carol pulled Sean's hand behind her. Exiting the banquet hall, they walked down the long corridor leading to the front of the hotel, where she stopped just shy of the lobby.

"Sean, lil bro, that girl looks just like, like Angela."

"No," he smacked his lips turning away from her.

"Yes, she does. Tall, light skinned, plus size, same length of hair… And you are still in love with her, and you are wanting to have her back so bad you are trying to replace her with a… a, what's it called, a look alike."

"Whatever," he smacked again.

"It's true. You don't want to do this to yourself. You really don't need this right now. Just trust me."

"Wow," he blushed. "You had to bring me out here just to tell me this?"

"No, numb nuts," she grabbed his shoulders, then spun him around. "See the IHOP across the street? All we have inside is chicken wings and finger food. So go over there and get yourself a large stack of pancakes to soak up some of your wine, cause you aren't thinking clearly, and then come back and give me my dance."

He could not help but laugh as he turned back toward her. "Are you serious?" He grabbed for the glass in her hand.

"Yes, I am," she pulled it back from his reach. "This is yours to take home. I'll keep it with me at my table until you get back. Now go!" She reached over gently pulling his head to her and kissed him on his cheek. "Love you lil bro."

"I love you too," he said as he watched her walk down the corridor. Carol was usually right about most things. Even though he could not totally see the resemblance in the woman on the dance floor, he knew that he could trust Carol.

"Arrrr!" he growled under his breath, turning and staring at the long distance between the hotel and the restaurant. "Pancakes?" he said in his *Tony Montana* voice. "We don't need no stinkin pancakes!"

The White party wedding lasted late into the night. Sean, never met the attractive woman, who had left when he was at the restaurant, but he did enjoy the party. Various light hearted single women emptied their arsenal attempting to capture his attention but Carol made sure that did not happen.

For their honeymoon, Carol and Mike had planned to save money to take a trip sometime the following year. That night, Sean, had handed them his package for a trip to Aruba. It was for the Soul Beach Music Festival that would be held May twenty third through the twenty eighth. Plane tickets, hotel, and other accommodations were all paid for. Carol, had thought that he had paid for it with the extra money made from working in Tennessee. Unbeknownst to her, he had purchased the entire package in October of the previous year, via a small loan. He had planned to surprise Angela, who had always dreamed of going to Aruba. He had planned to make it the best vacation she had ever had. She had always been afraid to fly and it would have been her first time on a plane. Many times he had imagined her squeezing the life from his hand as the plane roared down the runway and rocketed into the sky. He imagined pulling her close to him and kissing her cheek, whispering in her ear that it would be fine. But weeks later, tragedy had robbed him of this dream. Still, he considered going there, alone, just to walk out onto the beach and think of her, or take some memento of hers to toss into the water. But thinking of the ocean brought mixed memories of the bridge at the lake, which he still was not ready to face. Sean convinced himself that by not going he was letting go of her. While Carol and Mike would fly away to Aruba on what would have been his trip with Angela, he would be home rebuilding the broken pieces of his life. So he thought.

****

Near the end of May, with Carol, away in Aruba, Sean had relied on his own self-comforting words of wisdom. Keeping himself busy at work and packing his agenda each week with improvement projects on his as well as other houses kept him driven. Some days were entirely devoted to working on his book. But his house, seemed to receive the most attention. It was an older house, built in 1986. It was a fixer upper, which included two bedrooms with a full bathroom in the hall, a large master bedroom with full bathroom and walk-in closet, and a living room which adjoined a small dining area that led into a medium sized kitchen. No garage, but plenty of extra land space in the rear of the home, where Sean had contracted the addition of a large sunroom and an extra bedroom that would serve as a craft room for Angela. His experience in building and construction had saved him countless expenses, although, doing the majority of the work himself, had caused it to take longer than the usual amount of time. The house had been in total disarray with most of the old part having sheet rock torn down and flooring ripped up. The only finished parts were the completely remolded hall bathroom, the freshly painted Master bedroom, and the finished sunroom and extra craft room. Sean had been living with Angela at her rented home so it was easy to rip everything apart and rebuild without the constraints of working around or moving furniture or other valuables. When Angela was alive, it was a family project. Many evenings he worked late on the house and Angela would bring him dinner. Sometimes, with the kids, they would sit on the floor, laughing and planning how each part of the house would be decorated or styled. On the weekends, Shonzé and Alex had helped paint the new part of the house. Alex's eyes were always focused on every detail of Sean's skilled labor. He had loved to help hammer or drill whenever Sean had given him the opportunity. Sean missed his helpers. He missed his family.

Standing in the empty sunroom, he stared across towards the closed door of the craft room. He smiled thinking about its contents. The whole house had an echo because of the bare floors and missing furniture. When he had moved in with Angela, into the home she was renting, the plan had been to finish his remodeling, get married, move back into the renovated house, and be able to stop paying rent at her home. With this in mind, they had sold what small amount of furniture Sean had at the time. With Angela's death, along with the kids, Annabelle Stallgood had forcefully taken all of the furniture in the rented house as Angela's, leaving Sean to return to his empty house and an unfinished dream. But since November, he had worked tirelessly, like a building maniac, finishing as much as was possible for one person. He even finished the new deck at the side of the house -theoretically finished. The deck was usable with perfectly lain boards and steps that careened in small expanses down onto the concrete walkway. Corner and midway posts cut off evenly and topped with solar powered copper toned caps stood erect around the perimeter. The only part missing was the railing. Angela had seen in many of her house design books, decks and patios lower to the ground, without railings. She had begged Sean to build theirs this way. He had tried to make her understand that this deck was too high from the ground, therefore the building code would not allow it and he would be fined for it. But Sean had finished it, or half-finished it, the way Angela would have wanted. It wouldn't take much to build the railings. But until some inspector said anything, he enjoyed grilling and sitting on his deck, remembering the good times, remembering his family.

Hey Sean. This is Raven. If this is still your number, text me back.

The text message ring tone echoed loudly through the empty sunroom. Surprise and pleasantness flashed on Sean's face as he read it. He had not heard from Raven since February. He had actually given up hope that he would ever hear from her again.

Hey you. Yes this is Sean. Call me. Waiting anxiously, he took a seat in the chair at his desk. The desk was a corner piece, made of a steel skeleton frame with a glass top. His lap top and neatly arranged folders of book outlines, notes and a corded answering machine phone sat on top. The corner walls were actually the walls of the dining area, but now a bachelor, with no family or no frequent dinner guest yet, he had made the space his temporary office until the two hall bedrooms had been painted. The two adjoining walls were lined with papers and sticky notes filled with agendas, story ideas, and completion dates. When he was not working on the house, at his job, or the gym, he would be there, in the corner, typing continually, until his eyes were heavy.

Now, he sat, not typing. He placed his phone on the desk in front of him and wondered if she would call, wondered how long it would be.

The musical number of his cell phone played a few seconds later. *Raven Topeland*, read the caller ID.

"Hello," he said cheerfully.

"Hey you!"

"Where you been, stranger?"

"Nowhere. Still here, in Tennessee, but leaving soon."

"Oh yeah? Where you headed to, back to Chicago?"

"No-o-o-o, I'm coming to-o-o Georgia, to live with my sister."

Sean, sat back in his chair, pleasant imaginations passed through his mind. "What made you decide to do that?"

"Finally let go of him. I've been trying for so long. I finally left a week ago. Over the past few days I managed to get most of my important things out without him noticing." She Chuckled. "All the things I own, fit into my SUV... Hey, guess where I am?"

"Where?"

"I'm in Alcoa, in the Hotel you were in."

He swallowed hard.

"I got all your texts," she added. "I got all your messages. I just needed some time... I never stopped thinking about you."

"I thought you were still mad at me. Raven, I'm real sorry, about..."

"Save it. It's the past. You needed time to get over your past and I knew that, I just ignored it. I would like to see you when I get there, if that's alright. I mean is there someone in your life now that would have a problem with an old *friend* coming to visit?"

"No," he laughed. "No one in my life. You are welcome to come see me anytime."

"Nice," she purred.

It felt good to hear from her, finally. Everything was right about Raven to him. Sean imagined taking her sightseeing and eating at the many hidden cafés and eateries throughout the Buckhead and Midtown areas. But just as quickly as those thoughts excited him, he remembered that those had been the same places he and Angela had discovered and introduced to one another over the years. *Maybe going with someone else could help erase her*, he thought. *Yeah, make new memories.*

Over the days that followed, he talked briefly and exchanged multiple texts with Raven. She never told him a definite date as to when she would travel to Georgia. A part of

Sean told him that she would end up back with her boyfriend. After not hearing from her for a couple of days, he decided to leave it to fate and began reengaging himself with old friends. There was his tennis and gym buddy Kevin. He and wife Diane had known Sean for a year before he had met Angela. The four had sometimes played doubles matches, even though the only two who were proficient at playing tennis were Sean and Kevin. He also spent time hanging out with a couple of co-workers, getting to know his neighbors, and of course, cookouts at Carol and Mike's home. Life was mending itself. Time was healing.

A week after Raven's initial call, Sean found himself deeply focused again on finishing the house. With the air compressor kicked on, and his music blasting in his ears through the ear buds, he lined the hallway with and hammered down wood flooring. Amazingly, he could still hear the pounding on the front door.

"Surprise!" Raven's cheerful eyes and smile greeted him as he opened the door. A frown of confusion bent his brow, but a welcoming smile formed on his lips.

"What are you doing here? You really came."

"Yeah, I did," she nodded, smiling back at him. For seconds, which seemed like hours they stared at one another.

"Well, are you going to invite me in?" she teased.

"Oh, yeah, I'm sorry, come on," he stepped backwards. "I want to give you a hug but I'm sweaty and got all this saw dust on me."

Raven reached up and wrung her arms around his neck, burying her temple beneath his chin. "So?"

"So," he said pushing away from her, "when did you get here? You all settled in at your sister's place yet?"

"Uhh, not exactly," she looked away from him.

"What do mean?"

"I never told her when, exactly… I was coming. We haven't talked in a few weeks. I just showed up today at her house and no one is home. I called her cell and she and my brother-in-law are in Miami and won't be back til the end of this week."

Recognizing the familiarity of her longing stare, he knew her request before she could ask.

"You can stay here until they get back, but I don't really have a lot of amenities and the only other bed in the house besides mine is the sofa."

"The sofa's fine. I don't take up much space," she smiled.

"Naw," he shook his head, "you can take my bed. I'll sleep out here on the sofa."

"No, no, I'm just popping up out of the blue and imposing. I'll take the sofa. It's cool… Wow," she began looking around the house. "You really have been working."

"Yeah," he sighed "I like staying busy."

"So, how much do you want for me to stay here this week?"

"How much? You crazy? I'm not charging you!"

"Come on, let me do something. I'm good at painting."

"Yeah, maybe. I have to sand a few spots in both hall bedrooms and then they'll be ready, but I can't ask you to come here and work."

"No, it's okay, really. I've helped with remodeling before."

"Like I said," he shrugged, "I won't be ready to paint those two rooms until next week and you will be gone then. You could, however, cook me breakfast."

"Uhh, I don't cook breakfast for anybody. But I can do dinner."

Sean laughed. "Ok, why don't you do breakfast?"

"Well, my ex, I used to try to cater to him and do the breakfast thing. He never wanted it. Once, I cooked this big breakfast with everything perfect and he woke up and told me how stupid it was and a waste of time it was cause he didn't have time to eat all of it and how he didn't like certain foods. Then he grabbed a bowl of cereal and went and played video games for the rest of the day. So, you know, working in a bar late at night, I got used to sleeping late, and eating lunch or only dinner." Raven's eyes were watery and focused towards the opening leading to the sunroom, though her mind was somewhere else.

"It's okay," he spoke softly. "Dinner is fine. That's more than enough."

It was a Sunday afternoon when she came. The rest of the evening they spent talking and making dinner, together. It had been months since a woman had been inside that house. The only other woman that had cooked in that kitchen had been Angela. Though Sean enjoyed her company, it was strange seeing Raven standing in front of the stove and moving back and forth over the sink and counter. She was much shorter than Angela, but he could see a clear appearance of Angela standing in her place. *Dang it!* He thought. When would those reflections and vivid recollections of her disappear? Or would they ever recede with time as friends had encouraged? Or would images of Angela, the love of his life, remain in color, when all other memories had faded to black and white? Raven turned and smiled often at him as he thinly sliced small sheets of beef for the meal she was cooking. He could only hide his thoughts by smiling back. They shared similar pain, but they were both walking towards the light of the future trying hard to cast shadows on their pasts. Raven's strength in letting go and even moving to another state fueled his motivation. He believed that he could do it also.

Before leaving for work, he left a spare key beside the sofa where Raven slept. At work he scheduled vacation days for the rest of the week with plans to show her around. They texted and called one another throughout the day. It felt good to Sean, to have the feeling of someone home, waiting for him, thinking about him. Still, he could not allow himself to delve further into the feeling. Raven was just as fragile as he was, perhaps even more. All day, he had wrestled with the thought of paying for a hotel for her to stay. It was all so confusing how this new woman had brought up images and thoughts of the one he had not seen in months and would never see in life again. Even with the passing of so much time and his self-assurance that he was over Angela, her imprint was still on everything he thought about.

Walking through the front door, scented candles of Hawaiian Breeze and Desert Lilac stroked his nose. Closing the door behind him and glancing at the bathroom down the hall he quickly recognized the additional smell of *Pine Sol.*

"Hey!" Raven called, as she popped her head through the kitchen entrance. "How was work?"

"Good. You've been cleaning?"

"Yep. I like to keep busy too. Your sunroom is huge! It looks all finished. When are you going to put furniture in there?"

"I don't know," he shrugged, dropping his backpack at the foot of his desk. "No one's ever here except me, so I never think about it. Guess I was just waiting to finish everything, then go furniture shopping."

"Yeah, I can see that… What's up with all the puzzles in that bedroom?"

Sean's eyes grew wide. "You went in there?" he yelled. Racing through the entrance of the sunroom he bolted across the open floor almost knocking the closed bedroom door off its hinges. Stopping in the entrance, the door knob still clutched tightly in his hand, he let out a huge sigh.

"I'm sorry. W-w, Was I not supposed to go in here?" Raven fluttered, keeping her distance behind him.

"It's alright… I'm sorry for yelling. I just... no one has… been in here since Angel was here."

"Are all these her puzzles and stuff?" Raven had taken a step closer to him.

"Yeah," he breathed heavily. "This was going to be her craft room. Puzzles were her favorite hobby." His back still toward Raven, he surveyed the objects throughout the room. "Whenever I was here working on the house, she would come, just to be with me, even if she wasn't helping me, she just wanted to be near me. And while I was working out there, she would be in here doing her puzzles," he chuckled, "and trying to sew." Running his hands across the framed puzzles that hung upon the wall, he moved closer to the sewing machine, perched atop a wide table in the corner. Raven, had mustered courage to creep up to his side. She glanced up at his eyes, reading their pain. "I bought every last one of these. This one," he pointed to the unfinished puzzle laid out on another table, "was the one she was working on last." He laughed again. "I'm not into puzzles. So I haven't figured out what I'm gonna do with it."

Raven's eyes moved throughout the room, searching for an item that might bring positivity to the mood.

"What's all that?" She pointed towards a small shelf stand situated against another wall. On it were painted and glazed pottery items. Sean smiled.

"You ever heard of All Fired Up?"

"Sounds familiar. I think my sister told me... Oh yeah, they have clay art pieces that you can paint! I always wanted to come here and try it."

"Yeah, that's the place. We used to go there all the time. It was great relaxation. We put everything we painted in here on this shelf."

"What's that mean, on the egg there?"

Sean tenderly picked up a large soft blue toned glazed egg. On one side it read *MY NEST EGG*. On the other side was the phrase *CULTIVATE YOURS*. Taking the top off in one hand, a large smile appeared on his face as water welled in his eye.

"This was my nest egg. Inside I painted all of our names, the words 'our home', a dollar sign, the words 'hopes', 'dreams', and 'God'. All the things that were important to me. Right here, on the outside, '*Cultivate Yours*.' That's something Angela used to always say. She broke up with me a zillion times, and a zillion times she came back. She would always say that she wasn't gonna be one of those stupid people who thought the grass was greener on the other side. She said it was up to the two people in the relationship to work harder and make your grass green on this side; cultivate yours, so everyone will be jealous of what you have. Work on your relationship… Cultivate yours." Sean stood, both eyes glossed, staring down at the two halves of the egg. "I guess my grass was taking too long to turn green."

Dinner, came and went without many words. Sean managed to avoid eye contact. Raven, silently blaming herself for his reopened wound, relentlessly tried to entertain him. She offered to learn the card game he had talked about. She inquired about the many attractions around the metro area. He only gave brief answers, and in between chewed in slow motion, his mind far, far away. The taste of the Dak bulgogi could not stimulate him. The heavy spice of the Bibimbap never even made him twitch. To the broken hearted all life taste bland.

When night had come, Sean, alone in his room, lying in darkness, turned and looked out through the window, beyond the raindrops, past the tree peaks, and out to the stars –those stars that had kept him company so many nights without Angela. Those stars, had become his best friends. And within those stars, barely visible through the rain, he believed his lost love somehow resided and was there, looking out, watching him. Even with the tears beginning to cloud his eyes, with this thought came his familiar self-consoling smile.

Tap, tap, tap. A slow soft knocking on his bedroom door played with his mind. Was he dreaming? Was someone really there? With his eyes closing and his mind fading to unconsciousness he vaguely heard the door knob turning as the door's hinges squeaked and its bottom slid across the carpet. And if not for the deep echoing thumps of his heavy heart vibrating in his half-conscious brain he might have noticed the feathered footfalls coming closer to his bed.

"Angel?" he whispered, his eyes now fully closed.

"No… It's me," came a whispered reply.

Realizing the unrecognized voice had come from the conscious world, he awoke sharply, his eyes adjusting and hunting through the darkness. And there, on the right side of the bed, where Angela used to be, Raven, sat perched upon her knees and shins. The light from outside shined through the falling rain, making flickers dance on her radiant black hair and glimmers sparkle in her coffee bean eyes. Through the faintly lit darkness he could see the black silk camisole that hung from her sleek shoulders and draped flawlessly over her breasts. Without hesitation, with ease of familiarity she reached out and slowly caressed the tear tract beneath his right eye.

"Let me help you heal," her nurturing tone beckoned. And before he could reject her with words, before he could turn his head away back toward the stars, her lips were across his with warmness and softness. Then she rose back up from him, and as her long black strands fell against his face and brushed his neck, they both stared into one another's eyes. Her right index finger was now tracing the definition of his left cheek then gently following the curvature of his neck and down to his toned ebony chest. Her dark eyes, still locked with his, she waited for his response. And somewhere, in that moment, in his mind, he believed that he was yelling a refusal, but the sound of his lips saying no was drown out by the tense of his body saying yes. Then she lowered towards him again, tasted and locked onto his lips once more, and without resistance, without conscious broken hearted barricades to stop her, she threw back the sheets… and she took him.

Sean awoke to the smells of scrambled eggs, turkey bacon, Melba toast, and a hint of Raspberry mocha. As he walked down the hall, he could hear Raven's cheer filled voice belting out lyrics to a song. When he stepped into the kitchen, a full smile took over his face. Raven's back toward him with head phones and an iPod blasting music in her ears, she gyrated excitedly. Her long, black, silk hair bounced wildly. She was wearing one of Sean's short sleeve button-down S-A-T uniform shirts. On her small frame, it looked like an oversized dress, with the bottom reaching midway to her thighs. On the kitchen table, lay the buffet eliciting the smells he had awakened to, with two place settings along with juice and creamer.

"Oh!" she jumped, as she turned and caught sight of him standing there. "You're up. Did you sleep well?"

"Very well," he smiled.

Removing her head phones, she reached up, caressed his face, and kissed him softly near the corner of his lips.

"Smells good in here," he complimented.

"I try. You'll need some more eggs for tomorrow. I remembered you liked them scrambled... from when we ate in Tennessee, so that's how I made them. That okay?"

"That's perfect, but uh, I thought you didn't do breakfast."

Flashing a huge smile and her face overcome with a blush, Raven looked away quickly, then timidly back into his eyes. Reaching up, she kissed him passionately on the lips, bounced her eyebrows in response to his statement, and with a smirk she took his hand and led him to the table.

Among many places and activities, Sean spent each day showing Raven the small hole in the wall restaurants around the metro area. There was breakfast at Thumbs Up, lunch at Radial Café, and dinner at the Cheesecake Factory. Along with the many eateries, he took her to Olympic park, the Aquarium, Fernbank, and of course, The High Museum of Art. They even spent time painting at All Fired Up. They rediscovered the many common interest they had. They shared their various differences with one another. Each waking moment together was a pleasure that Sean had long forgotten. Each night was a comfort which he had not known in as many months. The summer had brought him hope. Life had brought more healing.

At weeks end, on a night that ended a day filled with more excitement, Sean lay across the sofa, his head in Raven's lap as she slowly massaged his bald head. The sounds of Joey Summerville played faintly from the CD player.

"Have you decided on a school yet?" he mumbled.

"Yeah, I thought I told you. I'm enrolling at Savannah School of Art, the Atlanta campus."

"That's good," he smiled. "I'm happy for you."

"Yeah, finally getting back to my dreams. I saw a few bartender openings online. Maybe you could show me where those places are."

"Okay," he muttered.

"My sister emailed me a part-time posting for Clayton State College. It's teaching beginner's art classes to teenagers on the weekends. How close is that campus? Have you ever been there?"

His eyes opened wide. It seemed that all the music and the peaceful ambiance resonating in his head immediately disappeared.

"Yeah, I've been there. It's about fifteen minutes away."

Alerted to his tone, Raven searched her recollections of their conversations.

"Is that… where you feed the ducks; where the bridge is?" she stammered.

"I really don't want to talk about it."

She let out a deep sigh. "Sean, babe, you really need to let go of your past. It…"

"I will," he said harshly. "It just still pisses me off."

Raven's massaging of his head ceased. Letting out another deep sigh, she slid one hand down his arm and clasped her fingers in his.

"You know," he shook his head, "that day was so jacked up. It should've been perfect. I planned it for so long and it should've been perfect." He laughed then turned over on his back and stared up into her eyes. "You know, whenever she would lie, she did this thing with her eyes. Her pupils would contract. She had hazel green eyes so it was easy to see. Ha!" He laughed sarcastically.

Raven, trying hard to smile supportively, turned her head and rolled her eyes then stared back at him. "What happened at the bridge?"

Staring up at her, the languishing of her eyes blanketed his anger.

"Sorry." He pulled her hand to his lips and kissed it. "It just still pisses me off. I just need to know why… about all the times."

Defeated, Raven only stared back at him in silence.

As the night grew late, Sean fell asleep in her lap. Sliding out from under his head, she made her way into the kitchen to prepare two cups of Chamomile tea. As she stood in the kitchen entrance looking out to the living room, the water in the tea pot slowly began to boil. Outside, distance echoes of teens in their summertime carefree chatter under the street lights mixed with the chorus of crickets and owls. Inside, the melodies of the jazz cd still played, drowning out Sean's loud snoring. When Raven returned to the sofa, he had turned to his side, his head now facing into the couch. She placed both cups onto coasters and set them on the glass coffee table. Kneeling down on the floor, beside the sofa, she smiled as she watched him and caressed his head, which broke his snoring, but did not fully awaken him. Then, reaching around him, she embraced him and kissed him tenderly on the cheek. And still in slumber, still lingering in unrequited thoughts, he smiled and spoke in his sleep. "I love you Angela."

When he awoke, the unfamiliar glare of a sun from a different window blinded him. As he turned, he almost fell off of the sofa. Searching with all of his senses, he failed to find scents of breakfast nor sounds of singing. But on the glass coffee table in front of him, between two untouched cups of tea, a folded letter lay.

Dear Sean,

You have probably realized by now that I have left. I think the world of you. I care so deeply for you. The first time I met you,

you were bigger than life to me. You were this strong handsome intellectual man who looked powerful enough to crush me, but inside you were gentle enough to make me feel safe. I would love to spend every day with you, and build a life together with you, but hurt people hurt people. I can't love someone who doesn't love themself, because you will only end up not loving me too. I can't ignore the signs. You need to get your direction back. Things aren't going to happen as perfectly as you plan them, no matter how much you try to control them. You need to learn to let go of your past. And when you do, hopefully soon, I would love to spend time getting to know the real Sean, who is underneath it all.
Much love,
Rae

****

The summer of two thousand twelve was hotter than previous summers, so the almanacs said. With Raven's brief existence in his life now seemingly lost forever, Sean returned to his mental labored lifestyle. With his book almost complete, his attention shifted towards planning the self-publishing and marketing campaigns. His break periods away from that were spent focusing on the house remodeling. With the inside painting complete, all that was left was the grueling task of the final landscaping of the yard. From the completion of the two large flagstone flower beds, to the widening of a poured concrete driveway and all the pieces in between, he toiled and paid his sweat back to the earth. Many evenings and weekend mornings were filled with building, planting, and nurturing. The small collection of close friends grew slightly, as he met different acquaintances at cookouts with Carol and Mike, or when he welcomed new adventures like rock climbing and scuba diving. Endlessly, he occupied and drove his mind further away from the past, from the hurt. That is when the anger began to grow.

Sean found himself reaching out to a deeper part of his past, still hoping to find answers to his recent. A long drive to the State Correctional facility in Sparta, brought him somber expectation. It had been years since he had seen his father. Though Sean had received letters almost weekly, he had rarely written him back. The long deserted country road, razor wire toped fences, and constant vehicle patrols infuriated him. But *maybe*, he reasoned, there was something that a man who had never been in his life could tell him about living.

Waiting in the large room, only a small group of visitors accompanied him. He had drunk so much water during the trip down, he had to use the restroom several times. Once, a boy, about six years of age, had raced ahead of him into the small two stalled men's room. Sean thought of his own childhood and the times that he had come to visit his father. As he stepped out of his stall, the little six year old stood at the urinal, his shirt pulled up high under his neck, his underwear and pants down around his ankles. Sean shook his head. He could always tell which little boys had male figures in their lives by the way they peed. Often, single mothers neglected the male observation skills or the need to teach their little boys to only pull their pants down enough to do their business without baring their behinds. *All boys need their fathers*, he thought. He wished the past six years, he would have had his.

"Boy, look at you!" his father yelled, in a scruffy smoker's voice. When he hugged Sean, he felt his father's hardened skin pressing and scraping underneath his prison jumpsuit like sandpaper. "Boy, you look good! Real good! In shape, clean cut. Hey Samp!" he yelled to the guard in the visiting room. "This my boy right here! My son, you came to see me after all deez years." Sean smiled, stared into his father's eyes, then took a seat in the brightly colored chair at the small table in front of them.

"How you been, Pops?"

"I've been good, real good. You know I get out next year?"

"Yeah, I know."

"First thing I wanna do is go see that Aquarium we got now. Heard it's the biggest one in the world. And when fall comes, you have got to take your ole man to see dem Falcons. They gonna do it this year, boy! I won't be out in time to see dis season, but I will next year. We got a team now, son!"

His father's optimism and excitement surprised Sean. His memories of visiting his father as a child seemed gloomy and grey. Looking to his right, he saw the little six year old, from the restroom, sitting in the lap of his father who was also dressed in a prison jumpsuit and flip-flops. The little boy's head was pressed tightly into the man's chest as his little arms stretched trying his best to reach around the man's body.

"I remember when you used to be that small and came to see me," his father gleamed. "You used to love your ole man then. Those were the good ole days."

"Good old days? You've been in here since I was three! That wasn't good for me."

"Hey, son, I don't mean it that way," he reached across the table and affectionately slapped Sean's shoulder. "I just meant, it was great, you know, seeing my little boy. And now you are a man, all grown. Bet you got all the women. Bet you a playa like I was, huh?"

"No, Pops," he shrugged.

"Yeah, yeah, you are, you can't fool me. I bet dem women be eatin' you alive. It's about time for you to settle down and give me some grandchillen though. You got anyone special?"

"I did, but she, she isn't around anymore."

"Alright, well move on. There are plenty of fish in the sea. You just gotta go out and find you another one, like how your ole man used to do."

Wow, he thought, *I drove all the way down here to get this great advice from the great Melvin Cole and he gives me the cliché about 'plenty of fish.'*

"You still working for the phone company?" he continued.

"Yeah. Got some other projects too."

"Yeah? You still into writing?"

Sean smiled. He thought that his father had forgotten. "Yep, almost finished with my first book. I should be publishing it next year."

"Well that's alright! My son the writer! Make you some millions so when your ole man gets out you can buy me some pimp clothes so I can go out and show you how to pull deez hoes."

"Humph!" Sean laughed. "I'm sure you can… It's not about money, Pops. It's about the art, the creativity."

"Art? Boy you are what, thirty-five, thirty-six now?"

"Thirty-eight."

"You just now finishing your first book? You need to forget about 'art'. You need to plan for the future. Get that money. That's what dem women want."

Sean faked a grin with pursed lips. *Thanks for the support and wonderful words of wisdom, Father!* he thought.

"My son the writer, or should I say Artist?" he laughed. For seconds, they stared at one another, his Father's smile never folded. "I'm glad you came to see your ole man."

That makes one of us, Sean wanted to say.

****

The vestiges of fall, two thousand twelve, launched China's little brother into the dark of space and into the darkness of humanity, uprooted twenty flowers and took six gardeners from the fields of Connecticut, and brought the intensified, already overly hyped, implications of eminent doom by millions of self-proclaimed prophetic interpreters of the Mayan calendar.

In Sean's small portion of the world, only the publishing and marketing of his book concerned him. Through various individuals introduced by Carol, and through networking via Gym and work associates, he had managed to establish an assortment of literary and journalistic contacts.

At S-A-T, he had been moved from the Construction department back into the Service field, assuring unavoidable direct contact with irate customers. It had always been the only part of the job he disliked. But with lemons he always had a talent for making lemonade.

"Hello?" a smooth melodic mezzo-soprano voice answered on the other end.

"Hi. This is Sean Cole, with S-A-T. Is this Mrs. Camacho?"

"Yes. This is she."

"I have an order to install a second line at your business location, Magic Cuts, in Morrow Georgia. I just wanted to let you know that I'm en route now and I also wanted to be sure that someone was going to be there so that I could access the inside of the building."

"Oh, yes. We will be here."

"Ok. I will be there shortly."

The rumbling of the loud diesel bucket utility truck broke the low pitched bedlam of shoppers and small autos when he drove into the parking lot. Quickly spotting the business address along the front of the strip mall, Sean grumpily gathered his tool belt and equipment. His loathing for direct customer contact soaking his thoughts, he armed himself with a forced smile and stepped through the door.

"Hello."

"Hello," replied the woman at the first booth. Acknowledging his presence with a smile and bright eyes.

"I'm Sean, I'm here to install a second line for you."

Never halting her work on the woman's hair in front of her, she motioned toward the front counter to the right of where he stood. "I think she wants it right there, near the other phone. It's for a credit card machine."

Sean hunched down and tilted his head to peer under the desk counter. "Ok." Taking his screwdriver, he opened the existing phone jack, and surveyed the wiring. Behind him, near the rear of the shop, an office door opened and tapping of high heeled shoes began their approach. "The jack's already wired for a second line," he explained. "I just need to get to the back room or wherever your main line…" Turning toward the hair stylist as he spoke, he caught the fragrance of a sensuous perfume and his eyes were met with bright blue stilettos filled with towering and toned legs of olive hue. As his eyes led him up past the knee length skirt, small waist and glistening neck line, he found a perfect smile staring down at him.

"Well, Hello, Mr. S-A-T," she dallied.

"Hello," he said, still sitting under the edge of the desk, staring up at her. "Are you Mrs. Camacho?"

"Miss. Call me Catalina." As she extended her hand to him, her curly black hair bounced off of her shoulder and the intoxicating perfume grazed him once more. He tried to stand quickly before shaking her hand but forgot about the desk he was under.

"Ooh!" she flinched, when he banged his head into the wooden desk.

"Ow," he gave an embarrassed chuckled.

Finally, back on his feet, he massaged the crown of his head and took her outstretched hand into his.

"Nice to meet you," she grimaced, watching him softly rub his head.

"Nice to meet you," he winced. "I'm Sean."

"Sorry about your head, Sean."

"Sorry about… your desk," he joked. "I think, I… dented it."

Catalina smiled, then glanced over quickly at the hair stylist who arched her brow and returned an approving smirk.

"I think that my desk will be okay. Are *you* okay? Do you need an icepack?"

"No. No, I'm fine. I bump my head a lot on this job. I just need to get to your internal phone box, where your main line comes into the building."

"Sure," she said. "Follow me."

Walking behind her, he noticed her smiling face in the mirrors that lined the walls of the shop. She caught his admiring gaze in the mirrors as well, as she made her way in front of him. The bright blue stilettos elevated her to even eye level with him, perhaps a little higher. Without them, he guessed, she was about five ten. Her thick curly hair cascaded to the crown of her derriere. The curves beneath her dress bore evidence of Hispanic heritage.

"Here we are," she turned towards him, soft almond shaped brown eyes and plump lips beckoning. He noticed the telephone interface on the wall behind her, but his eyes were still floating in hers. So mesmerized by the illumination reflecting in her eyes that he did not realize the sky was really being lighted by the bridges still burning in the path behind her.

"So, Catalina, is this your shop?" He slowly moved past her, still smiling as he talked, never taking his eyes from hers.

"It's half mine. Crystal, the girl you met out front, is my partner."

Stealing a moment away from her gaze, he quickly popped the cover off of the interface, inspected the configuration, and then, turned back to her. "How long have you been in business?"

"About a month. I used to work for a large chain and decided to go into business for myself. Crystal, decided to come with me. And you, how long have you been in the phone business?"

"Almost fourteen years." *Wow*, he thought, *it's been that long?*

"Longevity. I like that," she flirted.

"Yeah, it's been good," he said, turning back and forth from her and his rewiring of the interface. "Some days," he turned and stared at her with an air of assurance, "are much better than others."

They continued talking as he worked. When he had finished, he surveyed her from head to toe as she signed the work order in front of him.

"There you are. All done," she handed him his pen.

He looked over the paper work and without a word turned and walked toward the door but stopped a few feet short of it.

"So, what time?" he said as he turned back to her.

"What time for what?"

"What time should I pick you up for dinner? I think that I should take you to dinner, for denting your desk like that."

Catalina blushed and laughed in relief as she tore a piece of paper from the counter and wrote her number down.

"Here," she said, handing him the note. "You call me and tell me when."

"I definitely will," he replied.

"I look forward to it."

****

It was the evening of the next day when Sean called her; a Wednesday evening. The same sensuous voice he remembered from the previous day was the same voice that greeted him on the answering machine: *Hi this is Cat. Leave a message.*

The voice mail he left was returned about thirty minutes later.

"Hi, Sean?"

"Yeah, hey. How are you?"

"I'm good. And you?"

"I'm great."

"Sorry, I missed your call. I'm home, spending time with my son."

"I remember you told me you had a son. How old is he?"

"He's about to be fifteen. He thinks he's grown… But I just wanted to let you know I got your message and to touch bases with you. I'm going to have to call you back, but don't think I forgot about the dinner you owe me."

"Alright," he smiled.

"Alright. Bye Sean."

"Bye."

It was not until Friday evening when she called him back. But with her fragrance and the memory of her appearance cemented in his head he accepted her without questioning. He had invited her to dinner, Carrabba's, where he frequented and was close to her area. Catalina, suggested Fire of Brazil. He had picked her up at her home. She wore another fitted skirt and high wedges accented by a matching Gucci clutch. Had he not been driving, his eyes would not have been able to stop staring at her warm dark olive skin glistening from the street lights zooming past. They spent the night exchanging their history, though he opted leaving out his past six years. She was four years his junior, and had been married twice. She owned her home where she lived with her son. And though she had a natural talent for cutting and styling, she was considering returning to school for a nursing degree. He shared with her his love for art and his passion for literature.

A walk through Olympic park under the stars accompanied by ice-cream brought them closer. Saturday evening followed with dinner and a movie, and another walk at a park closer to her home. On Sunday, they met for lunch, and later talked all evening on the phone. Sean's mind was filled with her. Somewhere, but not too far away in his subconscious he wondered how he had ever lamented so deeply and so long for Angela, yet barely thought of her now. He still carried anger for her, but now it was only when he thought of her which became less with each day. During the weeks that followed, Catalina, replaced those thoughts. The past moved farther from him. Mondays through Thursdays he worked his secular job and in the evenings he exercised and poured himself into completing his book. Catalina and he spoke briefly during the week. Terse texts of humor and smiley faces kept them connected. He had worked so hard during the week that his time on the weekend, spent with her, was priceless. Catalina never once complained about him working so much and not spending time during the week. Some days, she never called. In Sean's mind he was blessed to have a woman who gave him the time for his writing, time to take a chance on his dream.

"I'm happy for you. I can hear the peace in your voice," Carol gleamed through the phone.

"She's everything," he exhaled.

"I'm glad. It's about time for you to be back out there. Glad you two are connecting. So, kiddo, when do we get to meet her?"

"Hey, you and Mike are the masters of cookouts and parties."

"Aren't you finished with your place? We need to break *your* place in."

He laughed. "Yeah, I still need to get some more furniture and…"

"Excuses, excuses! How about this Saturday? Bring the future Misses Cole here so I can get a look."

"Alright. Just don't be embarrassing me. You know you can be blunt with people. You have to give her time to get used to you."

"Me, embarrass you?" she teased. "Nawwww!"

Their third Friday together would be a formal outing. Martinis and Imax at Fernbank with an evening drive through the city. In front of the mirror, Sean smiled and examined his mustache and thinly lined traces of hair which could barely be called a beard. His eyes were clear and lively. Lines of aging had been slowed during the past weeks. Soon, he would be thirty-nine, though his youthful demeanor and fit body bore the appearance of a twenty-nine year old. His fitted suit accented his broad chest and shoulders. Everything was in place. But something, he sensed, was missing. The medicine cabinet behind the mirror seemed to open on its own. Beside the toothpaste, floss, shaving creams, and deodorants, a lonely container of cologne brought memories to the fore. *Very Sexy for Him*, was the only cologne he had worn in the past six years. But it had been over a year since he had applied it. It had been a gift from the woman who had dressed him and groomed him. Angela, had adored the feminine scent and had loved even more the male version which she had insisted he wear. Sean had never been a cologne type. He was a rugged man, always working in the yard, sweating in the gym, or covered in dirt and dust at a blue collar job. But among the many parts of his life she had accented and enhanced, becoming a nice smelling man had been one of those most remembered. Quickly dismissing thoughts of her with the anger he still clung to, he spritzed small bursts to each side of his neck. Deeply inhaling, he closed his eyes and found his smile again.

Walking through the romantically lit atrium of the museum hall, he basked in the attention as everyone stared at the beauty beside him. Catalina wore sparkled silver *Loeffler Randall* open toe heels with a shin length fitted sheer strapless dress. Among the admirers, envious females sneered at her glowing naturally tanned sunless arms, accented with silver band bracelets on each wrist. Her orthodontic perfected polished smile matched his as they walked arm in arm to an empty table under the Mesozoic dinosaurs centered in the great hall.

"A *Black and Gold* martini," she ordered from the waiter.

"And you sir?" the young barista smiled.

"I'll have a club soda," Sean replied.

Catalina appeared stunned. "You're not drinking?"

"Trust me, you don't want me to drink. Not tonight."

"Why? Do you get violent?" her eyes narrowed.

"No, exact opposite. I never drink so I have a low tolerance. One or two swallows and I'm the silliest person on earth."

She smiled out the side of her mouth. "Hmm, that can be entertaining. I'll remember that for later. But if you are going to be with me, we're going to have to change that."

"Is that so?" he playfully arched his brow.

"Yeah… it is," she grinned.

The tunes of Lenny Marcus filled the hall throughout the rest of the evening. The Imax movie brought opportunity for the two to snuggle closer in the dark. Ending their time at Fernbank with a walk to his truck, he noticed her enthusiasm had faded.

"Did you enjoy it," he asked.

"It was okay. I've never been here, so it was… something new."

"What didn't you like?"

"Oh, I liked it. Just expected more." She reached around him and tucked her head on his shoulder as they walked. "I'll have to take you to a *real* formal event."

The collar of her *Saint Laurent* jacket brushed beneath the side of his face and her fragrance caused him to ignore her trite condescend. A horse and carriage ride through the city cuddled with her, moments later, widened his nose even more.

"Sean," she spoke softly though easily heard above the clacking hooves of the horse, "I want to see your place."

The cool autumn air was instantly heated around him as his mind began running wildly.

"Sure. We can go now."

When they pulled into his driveway, the solar powered lights perched atop the railing caps had begun losing potential and starting to fade.

"No garage?" Catalina sighed.

"Nah, I'll have one when I build my dream house one day."

Her eyes rolled slightly but her pleasantness persisted.

"Here we are," he said holding the front door as he pulled out the key. "My place of peace."

Her eyes searched the lines and corners of the living room, admiring its quaint elegance, rummaging for its flaws. He showed her the two bathrooms he had remodeled, the made over kitchen, the majesty of the sunroom, and boasted over his mastery of every detail. Her heels kissed the bamboo hardwood floors as she toured the house. Stopping in the hall, which led from the living room to the bedrooms, she noticed faded spots on the walls where framed pictures, of children from a recent past, once hung.

"You have to paint here?" she inquired.

Staring at the familiar now empty spaces, Sean only nodded. A small lump squeezed through his throat.

"I know a good painter," she continued. "I'll call him for you, next week."

"Where's the fun in that?"

"You like painting? Come on, I'll pay for it. It will be my gift to your remodeling project."

"But that's just it, it's my project. I did everything in here. Yeah, I had help with the building of the new addition, but everything has my sweat and labor and mind."

Taking his hands, she pulled herself to him. Through the dress her knee softly arched into his thigh. "I understand. You are proud of your work. I get it. But it's just paint, hon. You've already finished the major parts, right? This guy could paint this whole hall and leave you more time to work on other things."

"Yeah, I guess I can see that," he sighed.

Reaching her wrists above his shoulder, she stroked the sides of his shaved head with the back of her acrylic nails. The familiar sensation sent a silent tremor through his body, making him close his eyes and breathe out deeply with a masculine moan. He in turn wrapped his arms around her chiseled frame and locked lips with her in what seemed to last forever. As her nails massaged and dug into his nape his hands caressed her long straightened satin hair, gently tugging, fighting the urge to tear into the back of her dress. Feeling the rising rate of his heart, she smiled and slid her lips from his mouth to glide across his cheek and moisten his ear with her tongue. "Take it slow," she whispered. "We have all night."

Sean awoke to the blinding sun coming through the bedroom window of which the blinds had not been closed the night before. Wishfully breathing in, there was no smell of breakfast, no distant karaoke, and no waking kiss on his cheek from a love of long ago leaving on her way to work. But still, he smiled. Catalina lay facing away from him, curled up with her face buried in a pillow. He reached over and brushed her long thick hair. His fingers felt as if they were melting through the strands which were softer than any he had known. Awakened by his touch, with her eyes still closed, she reached behind her, motioning for him to come closer. "Hold me," she murmured.

Sean slid his body snuggly against her well-endowed Hispanic rear and wrapped his arm around her, resting his hand above her navel, burying his lips into the back of her hair.

"Baby, it's eight o'clock. Let's get some breakfast," he said.

"Eight? It's still early. We've got all morning."

"I love that you are here with me. But there are so many things I want to show you, and places I want to take you."

"Aren't we going to your friend's house later?"

"Yeah, Carol's. That's at three."

"Well, we've got all morning." She twirled her body around to face him, then cocked her leg up and around to lock behind his calf. "Besides," she spoke in a soft sensual tone, "we're not done here."

****

"Ummm," Carol embraced Sean tightly. "And you must be Catalina," she added as she reached to hug her also.

"Yes. It's nice to meet you."

"Well, come in, come in…. Mike!"

A faint sound of a door opening was heard just moments before Michael rose from the basement stairwell. Closely following him were Carol's two grandsons.

"What's up man?" Michael beamed as he dapped Sean's fist.

"And this is Catalina," Carol added.

"Hello," Catalina reached for a hug.

"Oh, no sweetie," Michael pulled back, showing the back of his hands, "I got grease and oil all on me. Was trying to do a quick oil change. Let me wash up and then I can hug you."

"Then you can what?" Carol glared at him.

Michael started, then held his thoughts and turned toward the children. "You two monsters go wash up so we can eat."

"Uh huh," Carol grunted. "So, follow me," she said smiling at Catalina. "The food's almost done. Mike's got the fire pit going on the back patio. I thought it would be nice to sit out there while the sun is still out, and it's not too cold."

"That's cool with me," Sean smiled. "You okay with that?" he questioned Catalina.

"Sure," she said apprehensively.

When they stepped out onto the deck, the chicken and ribs aroma could not escape their noses. The large raised metal fire pit, centered amid the dusty patio furniture, blazed and animated the setting. Pulling a chair closer to the center, Sean sat down. Catalina, hesitantly pulled a chair close to him then spent a full minute wiping off the seat with a paper towel. Carol, looking at her in disgust, arched one brow and twisted her lips.

"Would you like a golden pad for your seat?" Carol offered.

"Carol!" Sean whispered, screaming at her with his eyes. Carol fought releasing a belt of laughter as she motioned turning an imaginary key, locking her lips and throwing it away.

"Oh, no. No thank you," Catalina replied, as she turned to Carol and smiled. "The chair looks soft enough."

Their dinner was joined by another couple; two of Michaels friends. Conversation was laced with periodic questions from Carol directed towards Catalina. Sean, tried his best to intercept the embarrassing ones. Catalina, to Sean's surprise, revealed her interest in becoming a personal trainer, expressing her intent of enrolling soon into a local certification program. By the end of the evening, Carol was convinced that Catalina was not right for him.

"What are you talking about?" he frowned, as he grabbed two beers from the refrigerator.

"She's not your type," Carol spoke in a low voice, taking a glance out the kitchen window, keeping an eye on the other patio guests.

"Why, cause she has money and is super fine?"

"No. Money doesn't mean a thing and I'm used to all the beauty queens you have dated, so that is nothing new... And *she* aint all that."

"Why you gotta hate?"

"I'm not," Carol laughed. "She is very attractive. Just seems a little too high maintenance and seems like her mind is somewhere else... I'm not saying. I'm just saying."

Sean, glancing through the glass door out to the patio, smiled at Catalina as she smiled and kissed back toward him.

"Lil bro, you already know, you tend to always want things a certain way, almost to perfection, and when you see a hint of what you think it is, you sometimes don't pay attention to all the other things you should."

"You just need more time to get to know her," Sean shrugged as he took a bottle opener and popped off both tops.

"And what are you doing? Cause I know you aint drinking that!"

"Mike wanted one. And, I thought… I'd try one. Never had this kind."

"See, that's what I'm talking 'bout!" she said as she took both beers from his hands. Quickly, she took a swallow from each, then handed one back to him.

"I'm not drinking after you."

"Why?" she growled.

"You been kissing on your husband! We're cool, but I don't get down like that."

"I know," she grinned, pulling the bottle back. "Now get out of my kitchen!"

"Aww man!"

November. The anniversary of Angela's death, brought no candles, no vigils, no reminiscing, and no tears. The only thing Sean had allowed to survive was the hint of anger that still simmered on the edge of any thought of his past. The weeks in between his Catalina-filled weekends were infused with his new found love of work holism in his literary career. With his home now completely finished, Gym visits slowed and personal projects were put on hold. Each day, after work, he wrote like someone who would die if they did not. An agenda packed with goals for each week down to each day helped him flourish. The publishing companies, the agents, the editors; all the hustle and run of hectic life. But the more stressful and congested it became, the harder he worked. And at the end of each exhausting week, Catalina, was always calling, always there for him to inhale her air of refreshment.

For her son's birthday, Catalina had arranged for his
friends to come over and celebrate during the day, but the
evening belonged to spending time with the adults and family.
Sean, arrived at six, wearing the black *Doc Martens, Hilfiger*
jeans, and cashmere sweater Catalina had bought for him. He
felt lost when he knocked on the door. He was greeted by a
young slender Hispanic girl with long brown hair. Her features
resembled Catalina, but she looked more Caucasian.

"Hey," he smiled. "I'm Sean, Catalina's friend."

"Hi," she smiled back, blushing as she fully opened the
door. "Come in."

A small group of people gave ease to his nerves. Most of
the family, including Catalina's mother and father had already
departed. The remnants included her sister Lydia, Lydia's
husband Jerry (the Caucasian half of the girl who had answered
the door) Lydia and Jerry's two daughters, Catalina's younger
brother, Noel, Catalina's best friend Mila, Mila's husband
Diego and their son, Diego Jr. And of course, closed up in his
room, Catalina's newly fifteen year old son, Marcos.

Walking through the house, Sean noticed the expensive
furniture and high end fixtures. The floors were mostly marble
with six inch baseboards throughout. The kitchen and bathroom
looked as if they were right out of an extreme makeover show.
Every corner boasted her extravagant tastes.

'Uncle Noel', as the kids called him, was on leave from
the Navy, and entertained everyone with his stories about his
travels in the Far East. Diego, who spoke with a thick Mexican
accent, picked Sean's brains on how to get hired by Southern
Atlantic Telecomm while his non English speaking wife, Mila,
focused on asking Sean questions which Catalina or Diego
would have to translate. Everyone welcomed him. Everyone
except Jerry, Lydia's husband. He had not really acknowledged
Sean since his arrival. He only sat in the middle of the crowd,
staring at the television, occasionally flipping the channel,
acrimoniously tuning everyone and everything else out. From
time to time throughout the evening, he would turn and glance

at Sean, look him up and down, then back toward the television.

Later in the evening, Sean sat on the end of one of two full size sofas while Catalina sat at the other end, her body turned perpendicular to his, her eyes and lips silently flirting with him each time he glanced over at her.

"Give me your feet," he spoke softly beneath the sound of the television.

"What?" she said, breaking her grin.

"Give me your feet. Put your feet in my lap."

"Why?"

"Just do it."

As she unbent her legs and stretched them across his lap, Sean took her petite feet and caressed them between his hands. Even through the thin socks she wore, he could feel the softness of her skin. Removing one sock, he began slowly massaging and lightly squeezing each toe. Simultaneously, he stroked the sole and pressed her heel, something he had done so often over a year ago. Angela, had taught him how to give her foot massages so great and so relaxing she would gently coo and fall asleep every time.

"What in the world are you doing?" Catalina barked.

"I'm giving you a massage."

"Um, baby, sweetie. I get pedicures and massages twice a week." She pulled back her legs and slipped her sock back on. "What you're doing doesn't feel good. I mean, that's why I pay professionals."

Sean, stuck in bewilderment, stared at her blankly.

"Looks like it's time for our weekly pool game," Jerry chimed in. "Sean, you play pool?"

Sean, now even more stunned, glared at Jerry before answering. "Yeah. I play."

"Yeah, go play pool with the guys. We ladies will be right here," Catalina scolded.

The pool hall down the street, was smoky and loud. Buxom waitresses alternated between the main restaurant and the pool area which was separated by a glass wall and door. While Diego and Uncle Noel played a game of darts, Jerry had selected Sean to be his first victim of defeat with the eight ball.

"You wanna break?" Jerry offered.

"That's cool. But… you got a problem with me?" Sean grunted.

"Naw man. Why you think that?"

"You haven't spoken one word to me all evening and then all of sudden you ask me to go play pool with you."

"Oh," Jerry shrugged. "Sorry, man. I just get tired of every time Catalina breaks up with a new guy, I have to break up with him too. So, I just don't waste time getting to know them or hang out with them cause they usually don't last."

Sean snickered as he broke the rack. "Yeah, well this is different."

"Ok. If you say so."

"Trust me, I know. She's just so, so passionate with me, with everything we do."

"She's Hispanic," Jerry grinned. "They're passionate about using the toilet."

"Hey, watch it!" Noel yelled from across the floor.

"Corner pocket."

"Look," Jerry continued, "You may have thought I wasn't listening, but I heard all the conversations at the house. I think you are probably a decent guy, so I'm gonna let you in on something: Ninety-nine percent of the time, Catalina, only loves Catalina. That's why Marcos is so jacked up."

"I thought they spent a lot of time together, during the week."

"Yeah, time together in front of the T.V. watching her stupid reality drama shows. And when he's not on the couch with her, he's locked in his room on those mindless video games…. Shoot! Catalina wants a Saturday morning boyfriend, not a fulltime one."

"What's that supposed to mean?... It's your shot."

"Meaning, she wants someone to have there when she goes out on the weekends or when she goes to parties or someone to be intimate with when *she* wants. But she doesn't want a relationship, not a real one… Banking, middle pocket."

"There's no way you're gonna make that… She's not like that with me. Actually I think I'm the one who's negligent with her time. I'm an aspiring writer. Don't know if she told you. But I just spend my weekdays with my nose to the grindstone. We get our time in on the weekend though."

"What! I never miss a shot like that. See, talking about Cat is a bad omen."

"No, my future brother in-law," Sean corrected, "Your bad omen was when you let me break first." He leveled his cue and with three calculated strokes sank his final two balls and then the eight.

When the men returned to the house, Catalina met Sean at the front door, with a smile and a tight hug.

"What's this for?" he beamed

Letting go of her embrace, her eyes smiled at his as her hand rubbed the back of his head then down behind his ear lobe. "I missed you. You were away too long," she chimed.

A few feet away, Jerry coughed and shook his head, as he walked into the kitchen.

Sean, retained her hand against his face then gently kissed it. And as he stared back into her smiling eyes, he enjoyed her presence, he cherished her air.

The days and weeks that followed had finally brought him to the close of his laboring. It was the middle of December and his first book was complete. The rough editing would still require his time but the main work was done.

A book release party, scheduled for an author Carol had introduced him to, was planned for a Friday evening. Rushing home from work and showering, his mind drifted in the possible networking that would present itself at the party. More authors, editors, and agents. More readers and book club members to socially survey. His life, in his mind was going just as he had wanted. With Catalina by his side, he walked with the bravado of a best-selling established author.

Stepping into the lobby of the Marriott hotel, Sean took Catalina's hand and pulled her towards the bar.

"Where are we going? I thought it was in the penthouse?" she questioned.

"It is. I just need to give you something first."

Her eyes followed his right hand as he reached into his coat breast pocket and pulled out a small case.

"Baby, what's this?" she bellowed before he could open it. But as he did, her eyes answered for her, as they widened with emotion.

"Just a little something to accent you, since whenever I am with you, you accent me."

"Awww."

A gold bracelet, linked in diamond studded hearts, with a floating charm of the initial 'S' glimmered in the box. Placing it around her wrist he noticed her ambiguous gaze.

"What's wrong?"

"Nothing's wrong," she swallowed. "Everything's great. I... just feel I need to tell you something."

Sean's breath jumped, but she caught and held his hand.

"It's nothing bad, baby," she persisted. "It's just that, when I first met you, I, I just knew you were married with kids and had two or three girl friends on the side... I just thought, we, this would be a hook up, you know. And here we are, here you are, showing me something I never really believed in."

His face frowned as he looked at her sideways. "What is it that you've never believed in?"

Taking a deep breath, she swallowed and blinked away the small tears that had formed in her eyes. "Love," she muttered.

"But you've been in love before, haven't you?"

"I thought I was. My son's father, I thought he loved me. He only married me because I got pregnant. It didn't take long for us to see we really weren't meant for each other. And the marriage that came after him was a sham. I was his trophy wife to be shown off and to stand quietly at his side at corporate events. Unfortunately for him, he didn't sign a pre-nup, so I'm pretty set for the rest of my life. And all the other guys? I don't know. It's like people were just there, you know?"

"What about your parents?"

"Please! They are just together because of the children."

"But all of you guys are adults now?"

"But now that they've been together this long, it's not like they are going to divorce and go start over... No one really stays together for love. People stay for children or business or other arrangements... Not love."

Sean felt sorrow as he searched her face. Slowly, he moved closer and kissed her soft cranberry colored lips. "Do you believe I love you?" he asked.

Wiping the lipstick smear from his lips with her thumb, she smiled as a tear crossed her cheek. Catalina held out and admired the bracelet dangling on her wrist, then looked into his eyes again. "I think you really do."

Rhythms of Neo-soul softly vibrated throughout the split level floors of the penthouse. A handful of self-enslaved starvation dieters hovered around the buffet of finger foods artistically arranged upon a large dining table. Formal dressed patrons mingled and networked throughout the night. Toasts by the hostess and of her guest followed by autographed copies of her book served as the highlight of the affair.

Amid the entertainment and conversation Sean had stepped out onto the balcony. Looking out at the city lights he imagined his release party and all its details. Smiling at the city scape and the sky piercing stars above he felt as if he were on top of the world. Turning and looking through the glass doorway, he was greeted with Catalina's yearning eyes and soft warm face staring back at him. Her ears were engaged in conversation with an older salt and pepper haired *somebody* but her eyes were locked in adoration with Sean. Motioning, in a gesture only seen by Sean, she called him to her. As he opened the glass door, the sounds of music and complimentary banter again filled his ears.

"...a lot of money but in recent months it's shown a steady incline," the older gentleman rambled.

"This is Sean," Catalina interrupted. "He's the writer I was telling you about."

"Hello, Mr. Sean."

"Hello," Sean gripped the man's hand. "It's Cole, Sean Cole."

"Well, Mr. Cole, I'm Walter Giordano. Your lovely friend here tells me you are about to publish a book of your own."

"Yes sir," he gleamed.

"I'm into properties and real estate but I am on the board of a large publishing company out of New York. This lovely lady tells me that you would be worth our time in considering publishing your work."

Sean smiled a glance of surprise at Catalina. "I'd like to think so."

"What is your book about?"

Sean hesitated, then quickly recollected the answer he had rehearsed in anticipation of that question. "It's about perception; how we choose to perceive things in life and how these small decisions affect our existence and our continuance thereafter."

Catalina smirked in approval then raised her glass of wine to her lips.

"Interesting," the older man nodded. "That makes me think of..." His words were cut short by the loud ringing of an ancient flip style phone which momentarily seemed to be hidden in one of his breast pockets. "Ah, these things," he whined when he found it. "So annoying. But how did we ever survive without them before.... Yes? Okay. I'll be right down... I'm sorry," he reached for Sean's hand. "That was my driver reminding me that I have to catch a flight. It was nice to meet you, Mr. Sean Cole. Catalina has my card. Give me a call and we can set up a meeting with you and one of our editors."

"Thank you Sir!" Sean shook his hand firmly. "Thank you!"

"Ms. Camacho, it was an extreme pleasure and the delight of this evening to talk with you. I hope to see you at my real estate seminar."

"I wouldn't miss it," she said as he walked away.

"Real estate?" Sean questioned.

"Didn't you hear him? He's into real estate."

"But what does that have to do with you?"

"Baby? You know I've always wanted to get into real estate," she said as she handed him the man's business card. "The market's starting to come back up."

Scratching his head at her for a moment, his attention was soon lost in the business card and the flooding imagined possibilities that entered his mind. *Veracity Systems Publishing and Marketing; Walter Giordano Operations VP.* To Sean, it was his golden ticket.

Wasting no time, Sean had called Mr. Giordano the following Monday. After a week of suspense, a company publicist had agreed on a last minute meeting that Saturday afternoon.

"Why does it have to be a Saturday?" Catalina protested.

"It's a last minute thing. She's flying out of town and the only time she has to talk with me is at the airport."

"Doesn't seem professional to me."

Sean, sighed heavily and stared at Catalina as she sat in the sofa beside him. "It's not some unknown or know-nothing company. It's a big publishing company. It was a miracle that I got this opportunity. And you helped me, remember? I have to go."

Catalina sat staring at her television. After moments of searching through channels she turned back to him. "This is supposed to be our time together. Business should be during the week… If you are going, I'm not going with you."

"What? What is wrong with you?"

Catalina turned back to the television and never answered.

"Fine," he huffed. "I'll call you when I'm done." Sean stood and walked to the door. As he opened and exited her front door he looked back in her direction. She never looked up.

Driving to Hartsfield International, confusion and anxiousness volleyed his emotions. He remembered the pain in her eyes. He wondered if by leaving he would become another reason for her to doubt love, to feign its reciprocity. *That's crazy!* he thought. *She is being unreasonable.* But something deep inside, some remnant of his past which had escaped through the wound left open by his own anger, fueled his trepidation. The night of the book release party, in the lobby, he had learned about her hurt, her hidden fear. He wanted so badly to make her believe that his love was true. And his unhealed wound, which oozed memories of Angela and what might happen with Catalina in his absence opened a little wider. He pulled over to the emergency lane of the expressway. In the distance, he could see low flying jetliners making there descent into the airport. As vehicles raced past him his thoughts became cloudier.

"Hey babe, It's me again," he spoke to an answering machine. This call, like the first two had gone ignored. "Whatever is going on with you, you can talk to me. I just want you to know that you are more important to me than a book deal or any business meeting. I can't go. Not like this." Gritting his teeth and closing his eyes he sighed deeply. "I'll be at home if you want to talk or come by."

The remainder of Saturday brought no word from Catalina. Throughout Sunday and Monday morning his calls continued unanswered. Sean's ride home from work was filled with uncertainty. But when he pulled up to his house, a new concern overwhelmed him. Parked in his driveway was a dark blue *848 Evo* motorcycle, wrapped with a red bow. Taped to its seat was a card which read: *Sean, I'm sorry. I love you, Catalina.*

He blinked his eyes and reread the words of the card repeatedly in disbelief. As he quickly dialed her number from his cell, he couldn't resist running his hands along the lines and curves of its frame.

"Hey baby," she answered.

"Catalina, what is this?" he spoke slowly.

"It's a motorcycle," she chuckled.

"No, it's a Ducati; a really expensive motorcycle."

"I just wanted to tell you I was sorry… for Saturday. I've just been through some things in life…"

"It would've been easier to just pick up the phone."

"But I can't really talk about those things now. I just need you to stand by me and be patient."

Sean smiled to ease his nerves as he straddled the smooth vinyl seat. "That's what I was trying to get you to understand in my messages. I will be here for you. You don't have to worry. You didn't have to buy this. I love it! But you didn't have to do this. This is too expensive."

"Baby, you know money is no problem for me. I just wanted you to have it. You'll look even sexier on it."

He inhaled deeply. "I don't even know how to ride one."

"You'll learn."

"How did you get it here anyway?"

"I had it delivered."

"You are too much. This is… is, wow, I don't know what to say… I want to come see you."

"I'm taking my mom on some errands right now, but I'll be back home later."

"Catalina," he groaned, "That's something else we do need to talk about." He could hear her exhale harshly into the phone. "We never spend time together during the week."

"I always text you…You have your writing and your gym schedule…"

"Catalina, my book is finished. The only thing I'm working on is the marketing and publishing which doesn't require as much from my brain as the book did. And my time in the gym is very limited. But I want, I need to have more than texts during the week."

A tortured silence followed his words. He could still hear her breathing in the phone.

"My mom's coming out of the store now," she answered. "Can we talk about this later?"

Sean sat upon the padded seat and leaned forward. He griped the throttle and shiny levers then ran his hand slowly around the illicit ellipticals of its frame. "Yeah baby," he agreed, "we'll talk later."

He wanted to show the world, at least his part of the world, his new toy. Telling his boys about it would come across as bragging to another man. So there was no surprise that he shared his excitement with Carol. Of course, he had left out the true reason for the gift. He could not let her know that he had chosen to coddle Catalina over furthering his career. After all, it had been his choice, and in his mind a temporary delay toward his inevitable success. Still, without knowledge of the entire occurrence, behind her genuine cheer of support, Carol's sisterly wisdom beckoned words that played on his conscience. 'Beware of the golden handcuffs,' she had said. 'Beware of the golden handcuffs.'

****

Fireworks exploding above City Hall ushered in two thousand thirteen. From the side deck of his home the fiery display was visible just above the tree line. Enduring winter's chill, Sean's bundled guests cheered and hugged as two thousand twelve faded into history.

"You're drinking tonight lil' bro!" Carol yelled as she held up a wine glass.

"You're at home. You aint got to drive nowhere!" Michael added.

Sean laughed then kissed Catalina as he held up his glass of cranberry juice. The muted television was tuned to Times Square. The stereo blasted hip hop hits from a radio station's countdown. With Jerry and Lydia, Diego, Mila, Kevin, Diane and a few others, Sean's first party in his remodeled home was wondrous.

At the party's end, after all had gone, and the music had faded to quiet relaxing melodies, he found Catalina lounged upon the sofa in his sunroom. The flickering red flames of the fireplace, projected a warm glow against her skin with her flowing black hair draped epically over the arm rest. Staring down intently at a book, when she turned the page she caught sight of him standing in the doorway, smiling at her.

"Everyone gone?" she asked.

"Yeah… What are you reading?"

"You tell me. It's your book. It was here on the coffee table… It's called *The Four Loves*, by C.S. Lewis."

Sean bit his bottom lip and cut his eyes to the side. "Oh yeah… I, uh, got that last week…in the mail. It was a gift… from an old, uh, friend."

"I was just skimming through it. I don't get it. Guess that's why I'm not into reading."

"But you read my stories right? The copies I emailed you; the ones that are going to be in my book?"

"Yes, baby," she squeaked, glancing away, as he slid onto the sofa, nudging his lap under her feet. "They were…good... Very interesting."

He smiled as he took her hand and kissed it, closing his bloodshot eyes and resting his head against the sofa. "Tell me," he lulled, "what parts did you like the best?"

Catalina slid her hand from his lips and caressed his head. "Baby, I've had a lot of wine. I can't remember all of it now. I just know I did like it when I read it… You are a good writer."

With his eyes still closed and his head sinking deeper into the back of the sofa, he gave an arrogant chuckle. "Yeah I am." Opening his eyes a few seconds later he perked up. "I'm helping Diego and Mila move Wednesday. Are you going to be there?"

"Wednesday? I told Mila we could help her Saturday."

"They have to be out by Friday. The only day Diego can get off is Wednesday, so that's when they are moving the big furniture."

The crackle of the fire filled the momentary silence. Catalina's motionless brown eyes stayed fixed on the pitch of the vaulted ceiling as her nails continued stroking the stubble of his head. "I don't know, she spoke softly. "I'll try."

Coming directly from work Sean met Diego and Jerry at the old apartment. Mila, had boxed clothes, dishes, and other small items throughout the day. A medium sized *Self-Haul* truck was parked cater-corner to the curb, aimed at the base of the metal staircase.

"Hey, my friend," Diego welcomed from the balcony of the second floor apartment. "Watch out for the grease."

"For what grass?" Sean yelled back, failing Diego's thick Mexican accent.

"The grease! The grease!... On the steps."

As he ascended the first stair case, he did not see any grass. Passing the first landing a small glossy spot on a step midway of the second stair well caught his attention.

"Oh! The *grease*!" he snickered.

"I told Mila to clean it up," Diego said. "Mila! Te pedi que limpiaras los escalones! The grease is still here! Caramba! Hágalo ahora!"

Mila quickly appeared in the doorway as Sean approached.

"Ay, Sean!" she smiled. Holding a rag in one hand she reached around his neck with her other and squeezed him tightly. "Donde es Catalina?"

"I thought she was here. Have you talked to her today?" Diego rolled his eyes and translated.

"No," Mila sighed.

Sean reached for his cell phone. "Let me call her and see…"

"No," Mila shook her palm at his gesture. "It's okay… Es Catalina." With a somber look overcoming her face, she walked past him and began wiping the grease stain.

"You ready to break your back, big boy?" Jerry baited from inside the apartment.

"Not really," replied Sean. "But let's get it over with. Why is there grease there?"

"I don't know," Diego answered. "Maybe the stupid neighbors, taking out their trash."

When they carried the sleeper sofa down, Sean noticed that the grease spot had been made larger by the wiping. He and the others stepped over it or to the side each time they passed it. The first heavy dresser was carried down with Jerry, the stoutest, on the bottom facing backward and Diego holding the top. Jerry slipped slightly on the edge of the grease stain but managed to keep his balance. The next cumbersome item was a tall armoire. This time, with Sean on the bottom, facing backwards heading down the steps and Diego holding the top, Sean navigated across the greasy area, but it was Diego, who slipped on it. As the armoire slid from Diego's hands it crashed onto the slick metal steps, amplifying the massive weight already pushing Sean down the stairwell. And there, on the middle landing, it slammed into him with so much force, the loud cracking of his bone echoed throughout the open corridor.

In and out of consciousness, he did not yet feel the pain from the deep gash in his chest or from his broken arm still pinned against him under the armoire. But his head throbbed from the blunt railing that had stopped his descent when he slammed down onto the landing. In between the flashes of consciousness he heard voices, male and female, calling for him, straining and grunting above him.

"Catalina?" he whispered. *But Catalina's not here,* he thought. 'You need to have direction,' Raven's words whispered through him. In a flash he saw a hazy image of Angela, sitting at his desk, slowly dropping her cell phone down to her side as he walked up the hall toward her. *'I'm going into nursing, but the Real estate market is coming back up, I don't believe in love, people only stay together for other reasons.'* "Babes," Angela called, "I'm shopping at the outlet while you're at work. I don't think I have cell signal there… I'll call you when I get back."…And then, a vivid, scolding recollection of the day at the bridge, ripped through him; an epiphany, like the paradigm shifting frontal lobe of a twenty-five year old, like the caterpillar's tomb ceding to the resurrection of a butterfly… he realized, but more importantly, he understood.

Bright lights blurred his already hazy vision as he opened his eyes. Mila, stood, with blood shot wide eyes, staring down at him, holding his hand tightly. To his left, a bewildered Diego hovered over him.

"Excuse me," a nurse said as she brushed by Diego. "You're awake," she smiled at Sean. "Thought you were going to be out for the rest of the evening."

Sean, took a deep breath as she replaced the bandage over the freshly stitched cut on his chest. When he exhaled, he noticed the throbbing in his left arm. Looking down at his new addition, a cast just below his elbow and down past his palm, he cursed under his breath.

"Urrrr!" he groaned. "Now I have to be out of work and bored silly for the next few weeks."

"Be thankful that's all you have is this cast," the nurse encouraged. "I heard that you had a very nasty accident. It could've been worse," she motioned to his head. At that moment, he felt pain shooting down from his skull to the bottom of his neck.

"My friend, we were so worried for you," Diego said. "Mila was so scared, she thought you broke your neck."

"Si," she added.

"Where's Jerry?" Sean asked, slowly sitting up and swinging his legs to hang off the edge of the gurney.

"He stayed at the apartment. He's watching the things. He called Catalina before we left for the hospital. I think he told her to come."

The nurse began listening to his chest with a stethoscope and rechecked the dressing over his stitches. "All the tests were negative, sweetie, but the doctor wants to see you first and run a couple more test and then you can get out of here… Do you two mind waiting outside?"

"Yes, that's no problem," Diego answered. "My friend, you okay now?"

"Yeah, I'm good," Sean groggily replied. His equilibrium was returning.

"I need to pick Junior and mama up from the airport and get Mila back to the house."

"Yeah, man. Go ahead, this is your only day off. You still have to move your stuff."

"Yes, Jerry's there, he can help."

"Yeah, go ahead. I… I'll get Cat to bring me by to get my truck." With tears in her eyes, Mila kissed him on his forehead and gently hugged his right side. She had placed his wallet with his identification and insurance card in a small hospital bag beside the gurney.

When everyone had gone, he sat watching the doctors and nurses zooming past him. Looking at his arm again, he tried to flex his fingers which were swollen and pressed against the cast openings. *How did this happen*, he thought. He had never broken a bone in his life.

"Mr. Cole?" came a scratchy voice from a grey haired short older man. "I'm Doctor Schneider." His German accent was thick yet understandable. "How are you feeling?"

"My head is killing me."

"Yes. Your friends said you had quite a fall. What happened?" Taking a small flash light, the doctor began examining Sean for signs of concussion.

"I guess I, I slipped on some stairs… they had grease on them."

"Grease? How do you know this?"

"Cause I *saw* the grease there… on the stairs," Sean said caustically.

The doctor smiled as he examined the top and back of Sean's head.

"So you saw grease on a step and purposely stepped in it?"

"No, I didn't purposely step in it," Sean laughed at the humor of the question. "I saw it, it was there, my friend got most of it up but I guess enough was still there. We were going up and down the stairs moving stuff and we just continued to step over it or step to the side of it."

The doctor leaned back and stared at Sean with a bewildered smile. "So you saw the danger, but you chose to ignore it?"

Sean dropped his head and chuckled. "Yeah…What can I say?"

The doctor laughed and patted Sean on his right arm. "Big strong man, more brawn than brains, eh?"

"Yeah, today I was. Never gonna do that again."

The doctor, still smiling, wrote notes on his tablet.

"You know, doc, the last thing I remember is, as I was falling, the first thing that came to my mind was why in the world was this grease there; who spilled it and why didn't they get it up… Humph!" he laughed then winced from the pain in his neck, "It was right in front of me; the whole time I saw it…

I was too worried about 'why' when I should've just never stepped in it."

"Yes, yes, we have to pay attention to the signs," the doctor tenderly admonished.

Sean's eyes widened as he swallowed hard and stared at the doctor.

"Mr. Cole, your head seems to be fine," he said as he lifted Sean's left arm. "And your arm will heal soon… Did you know, the wonderful thing about the bones? When they break, the body heals them back stronger. Yes! It's as if the bone learns and gets ready for the next, uh, not so smart thing we do, eh?" he chuckled.

Sean smiled in embarrassment, looked away, and shook his head.

After more tests during which time he had shaken off all grogginess, he walked down the hallway, through the large swinging doors and into the waiting room. His mind was filled with many thoughts, including the conversation with the doctor. He stepped into the middle of the room and slowly dissected the large crowd of muddled faces. And there, with a head lying back against the glass and an arm hanging off the side of the lounge chair, asleep and snoring, sat Jerry… waiting to take him home.

It wasn't until the next day that Sean heard from Catalina. The pain medication kept him asleep throughout the night and close till noon. When he had washed and eaten. He stared out through the sunroom's windows at the empty trees that lined the winter land scape. Squirrels, chasing one another, ran and leaped upon the empty branches. Sean wondered if they ever fell; if they ever jumped and miscalculated the distance or failed to grip the bark with their tiny claws.

"Hey baby," her mellow voice eased on the other end of the phone. "How are you?"

"Fine… Are you at work?"

"Yes, baby."

"I'm coming to see you," he said sternly.

"Can you drive, with your arm broken?"

Sean scoffed. "Yeah, it's my left arm. I can drive with my right."

When he stepped into the salon, Catalina greeted him with a delicate embrace and a soft kiss to his cheek. Other than Crystal and another employee, the salon was empty.

"Let me see," Catalina said as she gently raised his cast.

"Be careful," he muttered.

"Awwww, my poor baby."

"Catalina, we need to talk." Sean cut his eyes toward the other ladies in the shop. They gave each other curious looks then quickly exited to the back office. He took Catalina's hand and they both sat down in the waiting chairs.

"Catalina, I don't even care, right now, about why you didn't come help Mila and Diego. All I really want to know is why didn't you come to pick me up from the hospital? Why didn't you come to be with me?"

She slid her hand out of his and turned her face to the floor.

"I don't do well in hospitals... Bad experiences... I just... Can we talk about this later?" She looked back at him with water beginning to well in her eyes. "I made sure Jerry got you home."

Sean smiled a sigh and looked away from her, as he shook his head.

"Baby, I know," she petitioned, taking his hand into hers again. "I know I'm always asking you to be patient. There are a lot of things you don't know. But the one thing I can make you sure of is that I love you. I really do love you... Don't you love me?"

Looking into her misty brown eyes, she was still as gorgeous and physically flawless as the first day he had met her. Her genuine tears brought him memory of the pain she had revealed to him in the lobby of the hotel. From deep in his heart he still wanted to be that one different man, that special man, that knight in shining armor who would stand and defend her from the unknown troubles she carried. *'Hurt people hurt people; see the signs,'* echoed in his head. Letting go of her hand, he ran his fingers through her soft enchanting, flowing hair then pulled her to his lips and kissed her forehead.

"Yes," he answered her question. "But I love myself more."

Rising from the chair he walked toward the door, then stopped and looked back at her. Catalina's face was staggered and red, with tears flowing from both eyes.

"Goodbye Catalina," he said. Then, he opened and stepped through the door and he walked away.

****

Love anything and your heart will be wrung and possibly broken. If you want to make sure of keeping it intact, give it to no one, not even an animal. Wrap it carefully round with hobbies and little luxuries; avoid all entanglements; lock it up safe in the casket or coffin of your selfishness. But in that casket –safe, dark, motionless, airless – it will change. It will not be broken; it will become unbreakable, impenetrable, irredeemable…To love is to be vulnerable.
C.S. Lewis, The Four Loves

"You're a little rusty, but you'll be alright," Kevin teased.

Sean cocked a smile looking over at him as they walked through the parking lot.

"And this, from a short white guy I can beat with one arm?" Sean punned.

"Hey, I'm just saying, you beat me, yes. But not as quickly as you usually do."

"Somehow, I'm guessing, that somehow you thought that with one of my arms in recovery, you would have a chance to end my undefeated title. Come on, man!"

Kevin chuckled, "Yeah, you got me. I underestimated the Tennis talents of the great Sean Cole!"

"All hail me!... So where you headed?"

"Gotta meet the wife for lunch… Some fancy restaurant," Kevin frowned, then turned up the water bottle to his lips. "Ahhh," he gulped, wiping his brow with his wrist, "What would I do without her? If there were no women, men would eat raw meat, rarely bathe, and live in cardboard boxes or tree houses."

"Kev," Sean looked at him serious faced, placing one hand on Kevin's shoulder, "You rarely bathe now. And with the strong smell of DEFEAT that I just put on you, please go and wash before you meet up with Diane!"

They both laughed.

"Please!" Sean added as he slid into his driver's seat.

"Looks hot in there," Kevin responded. "It would probably feel good on a day like today to ride with the wind blowing on your skin, ya know?"

Sean faked an inaudible laugh as he clutched his stomach and slapped the steering wheel.

"I can't believe you gave the bike back," Kevin teased. "It was a Ducati!"

With a mouth full of water, Sean cocked his head with a smirk and shrugged his shoulders.

"See ya man."

"Tell 'D' I said 'What's up," Sean shouted as Kevin drove away.

He watched the image of Kevin's dusty sedan head to the top of the parking lot and roll out of site. As he let down his windows and slid back the sun roof, the fresh spring air began to chase away the accumulated heat inside the cab. Seating the water bottle into the cup holder, the glossed invitation cards stacked in the tray of his middle console sparkled in his peripheral. "Dang, forgot to give Kev one." With a smile, he held one of the cards in his hand then read the words out loud, "Book Release party for Six Senses, November 23, 2013. Come meet Author Sean Cole of Veracity Publishing." *Thank goodness for second chances*, he thought.

Sipping the bottled water again and cooling his mind, he glanced across the parking lot and up the hill through the opening between the trees. From the tennis courts, the view of the big lake had been blocked by the Athletic center. But there, in the parking lot he could see his place of relaxation. Tossing his tennis bag to the back seat he grabbed his book and walked toward the concreted path that edged the big lake.

"*No fishing or feeding on this side.*" he read aloud the little white sign which had been placed near the edge. Looking down the left edge of the lake he saw more small signs, all bearing the same message. "What is this crap?" he shook his head.

He sat down in a bench shaded by the trees on the *sign* side of the lake. Looking over his shoulder, the huge Administration building towered like an alien craft. To his front, across the lake, behind the scattered trees, the large concert hall cluttered what used to be a clear landscape. It was Saturday. But many people, including students, hurried along the paths and corridors between the lake and the Campus buildings. *College life; The hustle, the grind, the parties.* He wondered if any of these young adults ever stopped to even appreciate what was there, before the buildings, before the crowds. "America's future," he scoffed.

Across the lake, to the right, not too far from the bridge, a couple of students stood tossing bread crumbs to a large gathering of ducks. Sean smiled, then, looked over at the bridge. He felt nothing. There was no hurt; there was no joy. *Whatever*, he thought. *Whatever. I aint thinking about that mess no more*, he preached to himself.

"What are you reading?" spoke a gentle voice. To his left, stood a tall, flawlessly curved chocolate woman smiling down at him.

"Uh," he fluttered, glancing down at the book beside him, "*The Four Loves,* by C.S. Lewis."

"A love story?" she sneered. "You don't look like the type that would be reading a romance book."

Sean chuckled at her tease. "It's not what you think."

"Do you mind if I share this bench with you? I'm reading also," she flashed the book in her hand. "And I have some bread. You could help me feed the ducks."

The woman's smile, highlighted by the soft arch in her brow flirted with his attention.

"That would be nice," he smiled back. "The only thing is that they have these signs posted on this side that say 'No Feeding.' And you know how these gung-ho campus cops are."

"What?" the woman frowned, looking behind her at the signs along the lake's edge. "Where did those come from? So where can we feed the ducks?"

"You have to go to the other side; you have to cross the bridge," Sean pointed to the end of the lake.

"Oh. So you have to cross the bridge?"

"Yes."

The woman took a few steps past the front of him then turned around, "Would you like to join me?"

Sean smirked. As she stood there, he admired her lovely eyes reflecting the sunlight off of her radiant chocolate cheeks and maroon full lips. "I might just do that," he nodded. "By the way, what are *you* reading?"

"Oh, it's called *Searching for God*. Haven't really started it yet. I think it explains the difference and beliefs of various religions, I'm not sure."

"Interesting," Sean said, tracing his mustache with his index and thumb. "So, are you searching for God or a religion or what?"

"Just interested for now. But everyone needs some kind of direction, right?" She turned away from him and sashayed towards the bridge. "I'll be over on this side, if you want to join me," she flirted, looking back over her shoulder.

Laughing inside, he watched her make her way across the bridge, then turn to glance and smile at him again before she vanished behind a row of trees. And when her silhouette had disappeared, the bridge, unshaded and brightly lit by the sun's light, captured his mind once more.

You have to cross the bridge, the words echoed in his head.

Spring, is the time when what was implanted emerges, when what was old is tossed away, when what was worn is renewed. As he rose from the bench, three small ducklings swimming behind their mother flashed in his peripheral. Between his steps and the bridge two young squirrels scurried across the concrete path. It had been over a year and a half since he had set foot on the wooden planks or touched the pine banister. Hearing the sound of squeaking wood as he stepped onto the bridge, his heart went numb. As his hands rested on the rails and he stared down into the water, another face appeared in the reflection beside his; another time set itself free from his memory…

"Come on, just do it Angel!" Sean begged through his cell phone.

"What do you want to show me, babes? Just tell me?"

"It's a surprise! You like surprises! Just put on that dress and meet me at the bridge on the College campus where we take the kids to feed the ducks. And please, please, bring the camera!" Sean's heart raced faster than his truck as he hurried down the expressway toward home.

"Okay, okay, I'll be there."

The excitement in Angela's voice could be heard through the phone. He smiled harder than ever before. It seemed as if the short ride from the Buckhead shopping strip back to home was taking him hours. At home he could not shower quick enough. He could not dress fast enough. Grabbing the fire red and black print tie that Angela had bought for him, his excitement almost erased his memory to tie it. Even the drive from his house to the campus stressed him with anxiousness.

"Dang it!" he groaned. Pulling up beside Angela's SUV, he discovered that she had arrived before him. And as he made his way down the concrete path toward the bridge, he tripped slightly, scuffing his polished shoes. But with an insuppressible grin and his nervously floating heart, he reached his destination.

Angela was standing on the bridge, looking over the rail, down into the water. And when she caught sight of Sean, she smiled and turned slowly to him, her large green eyes full of tranquility. Stepping back away from the rail to fully face him, the faint shade of auburn highlights on the tips of her black hair bounced and enhanced her glowing skin.

"So what's the big surprise, mister?" she smiled. "What's it you want to show me?"

Stepping closer to her, the smell of Very Sexy grazed his nose. Her long black dress with orange prints finished off with her black heels, stole his breath.

"You are so beautiful," he began.

"And you clean up ok," she teased. "No, you know you are the most handsome man in the world, babes." She reached out and caressed his collar, then straightened the crooked knot in his tie. "You know I love this one. It looks so good on you with this black suit... umph!"

When her hands left his collar, Sean caught her left hand with his right, pulling it back to his lips, then kissed it softly. Angela smiled as her eyes began to water.

"What's wrong?" He frowned.

"Nothing. Nothing babes."

"You already know don't you?" he tilted his head and smiled. For a moment she stared back at him, then broke a glance away toward the lake, and back to him again. A single tear fell from her right eye.

"I know you," she sniffed. "I know you, babes."

Sean rolled his eyes and chuckled. Then, kneeling on the wooden planks of the bridge with her left hand still in his, he looked up into her watering eyes.

"Angel, you and I have been through so many ups and downs, so many highs and lows. We've been apart, we've been at each other's throats but when it comes down to it, we always have each other's back. We always come back together like your puzzle pieces; we've been broken but our seams fit perfectly back together. You've shown me what love is. You've given me a family. You've given me life. I thought I had seen enough, I thought I had experienced enough, not everything, but enough to say I have lived. But I didn't start living until I met you. I didn't start breathing until I met you. If life took you away tomorrow, I couldn't live without you. I'd search forever until I found you again, in this life or in whatever life comes after.

I know it has taken time. We agreed to get ourselves in better financial shape first, and I know mine took a little longer than you thought it should have. But what matters is that we are here now. I've loved you since we met. I can't live without you. Angel, I caught my first fish on this bridge. On that day I began my journey to manhood. I spent hundreds of moments here on this lake. We've spent many moments with the kids here. In mythology, a boy's rite of passage from youth to manhood takes place on water. This is no myth or fairy tale. This is our life. You are the one who pushes me, who introduces me to new things, and you are the one who drives me to working harder and being better. You, make me a man. So, on this bridge, over this flowing water, let our past wash away under it and let's start a new life from here." Sean let out a deep breath, relieved that he had almost perfectly delivered unrehearsed thoughts of his heart. "Angela Stallgood, will you marry me?"

Holding up the small black box with a diamond ring inside, Sean stared into her eyes, now overflowing with tears. Angela sniffed and wiped her hand across her cheeks, masking her hesitation with a smile as she stared at the ring. It was not exact, yet, sincerely similar to the ones she had shown him months before.

"Baby?" he questioned.

Angela, gave a deep sigh.

"Yes, babes," she sniffed. "Yes, I will."

Slipping the ring on her finger then rising up off of his knee, he laughed in relief.

"What babes? You knew what I would say." She mumbled through her smile.

"I know. It's just I was down on my knee looking up at you, and then when I stand up I'm six feet one and have a little half inch or so with these shoes, but with your heels I'm still looking up at you."

Pulling him close to her, they looked lovingly into one another's eyes.

"You said you love it when I wear heels?"

"I still do," he kissed her, gently tugging her upper lip with his. "And I always will."

While embracing each other tightly, slowly swaying to the imaginary music in his head, Angela stared at the diamond on her finger and began to cry again.

"Baby," Sean whispered in her ear, "did you forget the camera?"

"No babes. It's in my truck."

"I want a pic of us right now on the bridge."

"Babes, It's getting dark, it won't look good."

"Your camera is good. It takes great pictures. We have enough light. Give me the key."

Sprinting to Angela's black SUV, Sean never noticed the second scuff he made on his polished shoes from the same spot on the uneven concrete walkway. His mind so high, his spirits so soaked in levity, he felt as if he floated through the parking lot. Short of breath with quivering hands he fumbled with the remote. Finally, after years of uncertainty and waves of drama they were taking the steps toward forever, in his mind. He thought of nothing else, only her green eyes and juicy lips smiling at him on the bridge.

The camera bag was nudged out of sight underneath the front passenger seat. Pulling it out, a thin folded yellow paper, caught on the bag's clip, slung out to the floor. It had been lost between the seat and the middle console. Not escaping his notice, he glanced back and forth at it while he unzipped the bag and removed the lens cover. Recognizing the almost see through transfer paper as an invoice, he reached down, grabbed and unfolded it. "Delasantos Auto Repair", he read the company name. Weeks earlier, the SUV's drive belt had broken. With the engine timing being thrown off, major damage had occurred. Scanning the list of parts and labor cost he remembered the days when he had taken Angela to work or let her drop him off at his job. He remembered how calm about the whole situation she had been, considering it was normal for her to stress out about similar things, especially unexpected expenses. But she did not this time. She had remained calm. She had continued without letting it break her mode. He had been so proud when on her off day, she had picked up her repaired vehicle and paid for it and met him for lunch. 'See, like you always say babes, things always work out for the best,' she had said that day. Since they had both been paying off their individual debt and saving what they could separately, she assured him that she was able to pay for the repairs herself since he had been pouring money into the house remodeling. He loved her so much for the organization and the structured money managing she had taught him. She had given him goals and reason, direction and meaning... so he had believed. And then, he noticed the address and the name in the customer section. That is when his quivering hands steadied. And then, he saw the barely visible transferred signature, and that is when he lost his high. Matthew Franklin.

Why did she lie, again? he questioned. She had told Sean that she could afford it on her own. Was this why she had been so calm about it? The last time he had heard anything about Matthew had been close to a year before. Had she been seeing him or still in contact with him all this time? Sean's heart melted.

Folding the invoice back up and clenching it tightly in one fist he grabbed the camera with his other. Walking slowly, back to the bridge, his anger began to rise. His eyes, water blurred, but fixed on Angela, he moved with reluctance down the concrete path. Her back to him, she held her hand out toward the last of the sun's lingering light. The diamond shined radiantly even with the smallest illumination. Turning back to him, just as he stepped onto the bridge, with tears still flowing over her quivering smile, she spoke before he could.

"Babes, you are right. We have been through so much. But that is all behind us now. That's the past." Unable to see the pain in his eyes beyond the water in hers, she stepped closer to him and wrapped her hands around the back of his head. "I can tell by the way you never left me, by the way you worked so hard for me, for us, that you are where I always want to be... I can tell by the ring, that I will love being your wife."

Her French manicured tips massaged his stubbled head and gently pulled toward hers to kiss him but he slowly turned away.

"Angel. Do you really mean that? Is our past going to be our past? I mean, no more secrets, no more secret friends. We share everything, finances and plans," He demanded.

"Yes, Sean. I promise. From this day forward I promise."

Sean's eyes searched deeply into hers. Angela searched his face in return, wonderment showing on her scrunched brows. "What is it, babes?"

And after he saw it, that tiny flinch of her left eye lid and the barely recognizable condensing pupil, he closed his eyes, convinced himself that it was the excitement and her tears, and he kissed her. Slipping the folded invoice into his pocket his freed hand wrapped around and pressed her snuggly to him.

And there, upon the bridge, they held one another tighter than they had before…

Staring now, at a solitary reflection in the water, Sean had no more tears. It hurt but he had allowed it. Looking up and out over the lake, the crisp spring air filled his lungs. The warm sun felt rejuvenating to his skin. A hint of fresh paint grazed his nose. A splash off the lake's edge a few feet away brought him a smile.

"I forgive you," he whispered.

Then, jagged shards of his past surrendered to the serenity acquired through his journey and on tiny waves washed away under the bridge.

Looking out across the lake, he saw minnows near the verge, dragonflies skirting the surface, and two large swans making their way toward the beautiful curvaceous woman who was now tossing bread on the bank. When he stepped off of the bridge onto the path she caught sight of him, then quickly grinned and motioned him to her with her finger. Returning her smile with his own, Sean paused in his steps and looked down at his arm. For a moment, he twisted his wrist back and forth and firmly flexed his fore arm, clenching his fist tightly.

Love anything, and your heart will be broken, he entertained. To him it seemed weird though amusing his healed arm, with atrophy, was now smaller yet stronger than the unbroken one. Elated, he looked back toward the beautiful woman on the bank. "But it's worth it."

Starting in her direction again, with a swagger of confidence, the faint scent of paint and oil brushed his nose once more. Looking around as he walked, a familiar image at the auditorium's stone patio surprised him. Immediately, instinctively, his direction changed and he climbed the small incline toward the concrete veranda. Stepping off of the grass onto the patio, a kindred comfort overtook him.

Sean tossed the book in her direction, and it landed near the foot of her stool. Barely breaking her stroke across the canvas, she glanced in her peripheral, then back to her work with a grin.

"I see that you got my package. Did you finish it?" Raven asked.

"Not yet," Sean played along.

Trying hard not to look up at him, her grin began to widen.

"What took you so long?" she goaded.

"Uh… had trouble crossing a bridge."

Looking at him sharply, her smile dissipated. "Are you gonna tell me about the bridge now?"

He stared down into her longing warm brown eyes. Even without makeup and her hair tied into a pony tail, she was more beautiful than he had remembered.

"No…" he said, stone faced, in a humorless tone.

Raven sighed and turned back to her work on the canvass. "Sean, Sean, Sean," she grunted. "Still can't get over your past. Please don't waste my…"

"I'll show you."

Taking the brush from her hand, he gently clasped her fingers into his palm, lifting her from her seat. With a smile finding its way back to her and his eyes locked with hers, Sean led Raven off of the concrete patio and across the grass. And they walked, taking their time, toward the bridge, where another story would soon begin.

S. Combs

Veracity Systems Copyright © 2013

www.Scombs.com